CONFESSIONS OF DAN YACK

BLAISE CENDRARS
CONFESSIONS OF DAN YACK

TRANSLATED FROM THE FRENCH BY
NINA ROOTES

PETER OWEN
LONDON AND CHESTER SPRINGS

PETER OWEN LTD
73 Kenway Road, London SW5 0RE

Peter Owen books are distributed in the USA by
Dufour Editions Inc., Chester Springs, PA 19425-0007

Translated from the French *Les Confessions de Dan Yack*
Decorations by Yuri Annenkov

This paperback edition 2002
© Editions Denoël, Paris 1929
First published in Great Britain 1990
English translation © Peter Owen Ltd 1990

A catalogue record for this book is available from
the British Library

ISBN 0 7206 1158 X

Printed and bound in Great Britain by
Bookmarque Ltd, Croydon, Surrey

Contents

TO RAYMONE

B.C.

Le Tremblay-sur-Mauldre, June 1929

What can I add, Raymone, other than this
dedication? Your name is enough.

BLAISE

NOTE

This second book was not *written*.
It was *dictated* entirely into a *DICTAPHONE*.
What a pity that the printing press cannot also *record* the voice
of Dan Yack, and what a pity that the pages of a book do not yet
have *sound*.
But it will come.
Poor poets, let us keep working.

B.C.

Cylinder One

. . . .

The chalet on the Plan de l'Aiguille, 21st January 1925 – Why was
it called the *Pourquoi Pepita*?? I have often wondered. But there
was a beautiful sign outside, the bar was splendid, and I had such
fun there! It was, perhaps, the happiest time of my life. That cats'
orchestra! One day, on the boulevard, I stopped in my tracks to ask
myself out loud: 'Why, but why *Pourquoi Pepita*??' I had a sudden
desire to meet this Pepita and take her up to an hotel room. Just
then, a woman plucks my sleeve. She starts walking ahead of me.
She turns round from time to time to see if I am following her. I
follow her, on and on, and all the time I am wondering: who is
Pepita, Pepita from Chiloé? The woman who is leading me on
suddenly stops in front of a shop window and, as I lean towards
her so as to hear what she is saying, my eye strays over her
shoulder, over her neck, the bare nape of her neck, and falls on a
gramophone with the lid half-open: *His Master's Voice*.

I turn round.

The woman follows me.

Yes, but which master? Which voice? The little fox-terrier
obeys him, but Pepita?

A little further on, I go into Pathé. I go there every day. I slip a
one-franc coin into the slot and put the earphones over my ears.
The machines play, play, play, playing I know not what. I listen to
my neighbour's record. My eye lights on the woman, who is now

standing outside, in front of Pathé's window. I always choose the gramophone nearest the window, because I like to look out on to the boulevard while I am listening to a record.

The woman moves away, she glides along, she glides, she looks back. She has a face like the extinguished headlights of a car. Today I remember that she dropped something as she was going away. Why didn't I run after her, pick it up and give it back to her? I remember that I picked up the look on her face. She had large, beautiful eyes. But her look was . . .

. . . .

. . . Often I think about a whole heap of things, all at once. Why is that? I love going away. I have spent the night trying to discover what I should really have liked to be, in the various countries of the world. I should have liked to be . . .

. . . .

Everything.

This morning the jackdaws came cawing outside my door. For several days I have been able to hear the whistle of the railway at Chamonix and the squeal of the brakes much more distinctly. The midday train makes the most noise. It's a sign of rain. The thaw. One of these days I shall have to go down to Chamonix. I must go and find out which train I should take back to Paris; but I am not keen to go back to Paris. Not yet. There's no hurry. I shall go down via La Blaitière. I shall let myself slither down on the firn. It's bound to be softer now, with the thaw. I can't stay here for ever, filling my pipe and talking aloud.

The jackdaws are back again.

There's a gusty wind.

I am reading Mireille's little exercise book in front of the machine. I'm reading it aloud. I change the cylinder every time because I'm alternating them: one for me and one for her. I put mine in position and take hers out. I take mine out and put hers back in. I change them again. It's tiresome, and it may muddle everything up. I pity the poor young lady who will have to type it all out! How can I say what I want to say, say that . . .

. . . .

Sometimes I can't even fill my pipe. I have too many things to think about all at the same time. I have never been able to read. I don't know how to read. I just can't do it. Everything distracts me. I look around me. I look behind me and in front of me. I get up and take a few steps round the room. I sit down again at the little table in front of the window. I fill my pipe again. I pick up Mireille's little exercise book. I set to work. I want to say that. . . . I find a pretext to get up again and take a few more steps round the room. I sit down again. I get up. This time, to poke the fire. Then I go and fetch some coke from the next room. I fill the scuttle. I dawdle. I don't want to forget anything. But I am forgetting to smoke. I want to fill my pipe. My tobacco-pouch is in the big room. I go in there. But first I wash my hands. I light my pipe and look out of the window. I go back to get the coke. I sit down again at the little table by the window. I try to work, but without success. I should like to read Mireille's exercise book. I should like to say. . . . The jackdaws are still there. There are three of them. I go and open the door. There is only one bird now. He is sitting on the fence. Before he flies away, before he drops into the void, I still have time to hear the train whistle as it enters the station. The grinding of the brakes sounds much nearer than it did yesterday – no, this morning. It will rain tonight. When I leaned down to watch the bird, the bottom of the valley looked coal-black.

Down there, it's already raining.

Once again it's midday.

So, it must have been yesterday that the brakes sounded much nearer than usual.

I don't feel like going down any more. The valley is dirty. The peak of the Aiguille is pale, livid. No, it's not spring yet, in spite of this rain.

I go back indoors.

I am sitting at the little table by the window. Darkness fell some time ago. I am smoking. I.

. . . .

I did go down to Chamonix, after all. I wanted to post the first cylinders. I don't know why, but I brought them back up here. And now I am beginning again. I am dictating again, aloud. I am dictating into the machine, which purrs. I'm beginning again, but now I do not alternate the cylinders. Everything goes on to the same one. Outside, it's freezing, it's freezing again.

I start the machine up and rewind it. I press a button and immediately hear my voice coming out of the horn. I am reading Mireille's little exercise book aloud and the machine is recording it. So I hear myself twice, first when I dictate and then again when the machine repeats what I have just dictated. Tonight it's freezing hard.

I should have bought this machine when Mireille was ill. I had nothing more to say to her. Sick people upset me. I don't know what to say to them. I feel ill at ease and don't know how to sympathize with them. I have never been ill. And even now, when I should like to say so much, I don't know how to say that. . . . So I dictate what Mireille wrote in her little exercise book. I should have bought this machine for her. She could have spoken into it. And today I should be listening to her voice, her voice coming out of the machine, her very own voice, instead of listening to my own twice over, speaking out of the horn or dictating aloud.

Mireille's voice.

His Master's Voice . . .

How can I say that Mireille is dead? I don't want to forget anything. But how can I say it? I walk. Up and down. I light the lamp. I can't read. I smoke. The machine purrs on.

I, who used to love gramophones so much, am now excited by this machine. It's a dictaphone. A marvellous invention. Which amuses me and drives me mad . . . but how can I say it?

Mireille is dead. I promised her I would read her little exercise book every day and think of her. But I can't think of her. I can't forget anything. Everything distracts me. It's nothing. That's why I keep at it. I dictate and redictate and begin again and reread the same passages over and over and I waste the cylinders. I don't even try to imitate Mireille's voice. The machine purrs . . .

What a strange voice I have!

His Master's Voice.

I can't think of her, only of her. I think of Mireille and of Hedwiga. I suddenly think of my son. What is his name? The machine purrs. . . .

I have forgotten to press the stop button.

It was turning silently.

I am not speaking any more.

I should have loved to meet Pepita.

I often wonder who is the master of the little dog who recognizes his master's voice? What voice? What master?

Everything speaks to me. Me.

Me. I.

I don't want to have a dog any more.

I love my dictaphone. I play it all day long. Even at night. It can record sounds. The other night I put it on the doorstep to record the sound of the rain. I said to it: 'Listen, is it raining?' And it listened, and it heard the rain.

Night.

All night long.

I played it in my room. I glued my ear to it. So it rained in the room and all that time I was silent, I was holding my breath, I was thinking of everything - that is, of Mireille, of her alone, that is to say, no, of everything. Everything. Yes.

. . . .

Perhaps, by dint of dictating and redictating to the machine and repeating what the machine says aloud, I shall end up reciting Mireille's little exercise book by heart and articulating my own thoughts in between her words. I should record my voice reading Mireille's text and, simultaneously, my own thoughts like an echo, like a ventriloquist's dialogue. In this way I should have the impression of telling Mireille, in my turn, everything that distracted me as I listened to myself.

I could say anything I liked to her, no matter what, and I could always make her laugh. I have always been happy. Everything amuses me. And now that I am amusing myself with the dictaphone, she is dead. And I loved Mireille precisely because everything I gave her, everything I was able to do for her, everything I told her, amused her. God, how we used to laugh together! She could never take me seriously. I could say anything to her, without reservation and, what was more, laugh with a light heart. It was the first time! And Mireille, too, laughed and laughed with all her heart. Ah! If only I had her laugh and mine on the machine! There was no malice between us. It was all love.

For instance, I wanted to be a driving instructor. I told Mireille about it. How amusing, to teach people to drive! Driving lessons take place in deserted districts that are unlike all others. Have you noticed that the houses are there only as scenery, and that the boulevard is specially arranged so as to make an obstacle-course? There are queues of buses at the stop, there are some men wheeling barrows about, a tram turning in the wrong direction, a cyclist coolly practising trick cycling. Beware! It's a frame-up, and as soon as the ridiculous little car from the motoring school arrives, all hell will break loose. Look out! The little car is coming, it stops for no reason, jerks forward in fits and starts, runs backwards, turns, shoots off again because the beginner who is crouched over the wheel still knows nothing about speed and presses the accelerator with all his might, thinking it is the brake. He feels as if he's in an aeroplane! The giddier he feels, the livelier the street becomes. The little car sounds its horn all by itself. The driving instructor gesticulates wildly. Everything is moving like an express train, playing leap-frog, and it is at this precise moment that the one and only pedestrian decides to dash across the road and throw himself in front of the car. One day I saw a passer-by crash through a huge advertisement for *Bébé Cadum* soap, and the little car from the motoring school fly down the steps to the Métro, so as to avoid colliding with one another. Yet there's never any damage. One would think it's all arranged in advance, and that, like a clockwork toy, it's all wound up again every morning. Another time, on the boulevard Péreire, Mireille pointed out Monsieur de Max, of the Comédie-Française, to me. He was learning to drive. Mireille knew everybody. I pointed another man out to Mireille.

'And that gentleman there, isn't he the President of the Republic, taking a lesson incognito?'

'It looks very much like him, but it's not him, it's the Director of the Institute for the Deaf and Dumb, it's Monsieur . . .'

'Ah! I see. So that's why he forgets to sound his horn and has his headlights on!'

Mireille and I burst out laughing.

Everything amused us.

Paris is as big as the four corners of the earth. One day I shall go and live in the quartier Montsouris, which is like the countryside in England, in my country. At the corner of the street, there's a cluster of pine trees with a carpet of pine needles spread over the cobbles. Even the noise of the big dust-carts which pass that way is absorbed by this carpet; you'd think the engine had gone underground and was emitting, not a cloud of stinking petrol and the foul smell of garbage, but a sweet odour of crushed resin. That's where I shall go and live with my son.

Today is the 7th.

. . . .

Cylinder Two

. . . .
. . . . . Mademoiselle, ...
be very careful, this cylinder is cracked. I don't want you to think
it's my voice that's trembling, or that I have a speech impediment,
it's just that the cylinder is cracked. It slipped out of my hand. I
dropped it. It's split from end to end. Be very careful. As for my
English accent, it's not so pronounced as to make my speech
incomprehensible. You can judge for yourself, Mademoiselle. But
I have recited Mireille's little exercise book so often, so many
hundreds of times, that sometimes I no longer know what I'm
saying, or even whether I am silent or thinking out loud. I knew it
so well by heart that I no longer thought about what I was saying
into the machine and I began to think of other things. Well, you'll
see for yourself. I am sending you this cracked cylinder because it
is the most complete. From every point of view.

I have slipped a blank cheque into the cylinder. You can get it
out quite easily with your fingers or with a pencil. Forgive me,
Mademoiselle, I do so enjoy giving pleasure; so you will, won't you,
be good enough to go and buy yourself something? Some
fashionable bit of nonsense, a folding umbrella, a little dress, a
little hat, or a bottle of scent. It would make me so happy. Or, if
you smoke, you might like the Dunhill lighter, it's a charming
thing and doesn't hurt your fingers, or the Erméto watch - they
make them in the Chinese style, and you can find them in any of

the boutiques on the rue de la Paix. If you prefer beauty products, go and see my friend, Dr Ferral, 102 rue de l'Université, who has the best products in the world, cosmetics, creams, lotions, lipsticks; go and see him, he's a charming man, he will make up special products just for you, to suit your skin. Thank you. And forgive me.

You could also put yourself in Ferral's hands for a rejuvenating treatment. But you are young, aren't you? You are a typist. A delightful job. I should like to be a typist. If I were a woman, I should like to be a tram-driver in a working-class district, or a touring actress. Yes, Sarah Bernhardt. Or no, a famous dancer – yes, I'd rather be a dancer. But to be a tram-driver! It's like being captain of a ship but still free to swear like a sailor. And I should enjoy clearing the road in front of my tram by playing an operatic aria on my klaxon. I know one – her name's not Pepita – who is a real virago, savage, always grinning; she drives a ridiculous little buttercup-yellow tram, perched up high on its wheels, around the port in Malaga, and, oh yes, she plays fandangoes on her bell, and when she crosses the Calle Mayor, she drives her tram slowly, or like an express train, according to the tune that's running through her head, just as one guides one's dancing partner fast or slow, according to the tempo of the music, when *one is mad about her*!

Don't laugh at me, Mademoiselle, I am garrulous, like all my compatriots. On the Continent people think the English are taciturn. But don't you believe it. When the Englishman is silent amongst his fellow men, it means he is soliloquizing silently to himself. It is this ratiocination which makes every Englishman look like a disagreeable old maid. At heart, the man is compassionate. Everyone in England talks nonsense. If you like the gramophone, I shall have the latest records sent to you, but what do you think of this machine, Mademoiselle? For me, the dictaphone is an apparatus that awakens every echo.

'I love you!' I make it say. Then I make it say it again, faster or slower: 'I l'v y'u!' and 'IIIIIIIIllllllllloooooooovvvvvvvvveeeeeeeeyyyyyyyyooooooooouuuuuuuu!'

Sometimes I stuff blotting-paper into the horn and listen to it speaking through its nose and stammering this phrase in the funniest, or the most tragic way. I can also play with the voltage,

17

or make crescendos and decrescendos by tickling the diaphragm. What do joy and sorrow depend on? On the pressure of a finger on a spring! It's irresistible.

Don't let this stop you from going to Chanel to choose the most beautiful dress, Mademoiselle. Mention my name. Chanel is a friend of mine. She made a lot of dresses for me when I was producing films. I must also confess to you now that I, too - it was years and years ago, but I still haven't forgotten it - one day, I, too, found a little piece of paper stuffed into a tube, but it wasn't a cheque inside a wax cylinder, it was a letter from a woman, stuffed into a cigarette-holder. It was hard to get it out. The cigarette-holder was made of amber and richly inlaid with gold and precious gems; I don't even know what I did with it. As for the little crumpled letter, it changed my life. Afterwards. . . . But you will see in due course.

So, let me be brief.

Here are my recommendations, Mademoiselle. The cylinders on which I've recorded Mireille's little exercise book are damaged. As I said. One slipped out of my hand, the second is scratched, the third is almost unintelligible because . . . because I don't know how to read, still less how to read aloud. Besides, very often I started whistling so as to think of other things, or, thinking of other things, I started whistling or singing or talking aloud about other things. As you know, the machine records everything. I can't make head or tail of it any more. So you will have to disentangle it yourself. Mademoiselle, with this you will find the text of Mireille's exercise book. Would you be so kind as to refer to it as often as possible, so as to reconstitute it in its entirety, and take no notice of all the things I've added or omitted. Don't type out my comments, or my interpolations, or my whistling, or my stammerings. There's no need. And don't lose this little exercise book. It's just a little school exercise book, with the multiplication tables on the back. I bought it at the corner shop. Mireille wrote it at Saint-Gervais one spring. I am very fond of it. Please be so kind as to send it back to me with a photograph of yourself . . . .
. . . . . . Perhaps you know, Mademoiselle, that Mireille is dead? . . . . That is what I wanted

18

to tell you . . . .
. . . .
. . . . Yes . . . .
. . . .

Cylinder Two (B)

Mireille's Little Exercise Book

. . . .

Perched on two chairs and wearing a white cambric dress, Mireille is rehearsing the *Saint-Auguste* she must sing to her father to wish him a happy name-day. She is holding a big bunch of marvel of Peru in each of her little hands. She curtsies and sings:

> Papa dear, papa dear,
> It's your name-day today,
> I've picked you some flowers
> To make a nosegay.

and every day recalls a lovely day in childhood.

Another time.

She is taken to the old church: 'Monsieur le Curé, Mireille didn't want to come, and she must confess. Tell Monsieur le Curé your sins – go on, tell him! Very well then, I shall tell them for her. Monsieur le Curé, she steals sugar from the kitchen and doesn't even put the lid back on the sugar-basin. That's how we know she's been at it. The maid teaches her rude words, she says the Sisters are all cows and turds!'

Another day she is supposed to act in a nativity play. They teach the little Mireille to cross herself with her right hand. She persists in doing it with her left hand. The Monseigneur arrives at the convent. The Baby Jesus is in the manger. (Mireille is playing the part of Jesus in the play.) She is naked, and, at the moment of the blessing, she again crosses herself with her left hand. Monseigneur scolds her gently. What an innocent little thing!

She goes to the Sainte-Baume, to Simiane and to Roquefavour, where there are beautiful walks. She goes with her grandmother. Grandmother is taking her to see the Holy Relics at Saint-Sauveur. Afterwards they are going to eat at Aunt Marie's. Aunt Marie is very fat and she hands out slices of beautiful golden bread. Aunt Marie is busy in the kitchen, preparing the chocolate. They hear her fall. Mireille runs in to see what has happened. Aunt Marie is lying there like an old boat beached on its side. She is dead. How funny Aunt Marie's death is! They run lighted candles over her hands. No response, it's really the end, that's it, she will never move again. That evening, Mireille is sent to sleep at Marie Febron's house. She would have liked to stay there.

Now, I remember nothing of all that. Now I am in the country, every day!

What beautiful days!

On Sundays we go to see Aunt Marie in the cemetery. Someone has lent me a little watering-can and I water the grave and sweep the paths with a little broom made of small cypress branches. While grandmother visits other graves, I run quickly to the gardener's lodge. Behind it there are three abandoned graves which he cultivates. Artichokes bigger than my head grow there - honestly, I measured them, they were bigger than my head! Grandmother teaches me to spin. What glorious days, so hot, so long! When Mamma comes to see me, they stuff me with chocolates so that I won't cry.

I forget so much, so many things. I remember that Papa loved to have me with him. Always. As often as possible. And I too loved going out with him.

'When you're a big girl, we'll get into two big sacks and have ourselves loaded on to a sailing-ship,' he used to say to me. 'So, the two of us will sail away together.'

That's what Papa said we would do when I was a big girl.

Meanwhile, we go out every morning in the gig. Papa does his rounds as a country doctor. At Roquevaire, at Bouilladisse, at Puits-Léonie, at Saint-Pons, at Les Milles, at Barque-Fuveau, at

Septèmes, at Simiane, at Luynes, at Pey-Blanc, at Les Aygalades, everywhere, there are sick people waiting for him. Agitated women who have neither washed their faces nor combed their hair, and who all have stomach-aches, children with pimples and scabs, bed-ridden people, men who do not go to work, a baby who lies without moving, whimpering old men, a lot of nasty old women who cry. As for me, I am not afraid, because Papa is always gay. He sings, or he whistles through his teeth, and I am happy, happy to be mixed up in all these things, and to unwind bandages and lint. When we come back, I am usually carrying a couple of pigeons in a basket, or a fine hen that's terrified of me, or fruit, butter, eggs, vegetables, or a bunch of flowers that the good people have given us. The country folk give Papa all sorts of things, because everyone loves him, my papa. Me, too, and I am very proud. Only, I don't understand why he dawdles on the way back, stops at the slightest excuse, starts telling me a story and is never in a hurry to get home. But I'm hungry.

Now, I am already a big girl. I don't plant sausages in front of the house any more, as my little cousin, Félicien, told me to do, because I know now that sausages don't grow.

I have my own little garden. I pull out the weeds. I water it. I sow sous and anything that comes to hand, once, even the head of my doll. That dear little garden I had as a child, how I love it, even today! I sowed all the sous out of my money-box there, and I sowed all my memories there! Félicien unearthed all the sous, behind me, and I didn't even notice, but my memories are still there in the garden. I wonder if the children of the new owner have ever unearthed them?

My little garden was in front of the house. One fine day they brought a miner on a wheelbarrow. He had driven his pickaxe into his head. I ran into the kitchen to fetch him a glass of old marc. I was hoping to see him sit up and pull that pickaxe out of his head himself. When I came back, Papa and the men were bustling round the wounded man. Everyone was shouting. I was sent away. Papa was angry. That was the first time. In revenge, I drank the glass I was still holding in my hand and went upstairs to bed. I sulked, I felt sick, I fell asleep.

I am at Aunt Fanny's house in Riez. Her house is under a big

22

bridge. You go in through a granary. The granary is full of manure. We took the coach to get there, then the train, then another coach to Valensole, and then - there you are at Riez. How lovely it smells, with the lilacs under the colonnades of the bridge! Aunt Fanny's house is much too big for her. Aunt Fanny is much too small for her house. It smells of mildew and she lives there all alone, with an old servant called Marie who never goes to bed. Marie is never amused. The two old women never go out. When they eat, Aunt Fanny pounds her cheese and nuts in a mortar, then she pours her soup over it all and eats it. Marie, the maid, has nothing but a big plate of soup. They never give her nuts or cheese. Nor does she have a little mortar. They eat with wooden spoons. The two old women drink a bottle of good red wine, and in the evening, before putting out the lights, a small glass of old Chartreuse. They eat only one meal a day, but they munch fritters all day long, fritters with honey.

On the staircase there's a thick rope that serves as a handrail. The whole house is disused. The hen-house is on the fifth floor and there are two rabbits and a guinea-pig in the drawing-room. The beehives are on the balcony of a big corner room on the third floor. It is on this balcony that a little choirboy teaches me the song 'Come along, my chick, come along, my chick, come along!' while processions pass down the street, or wedding parties are held behind garden walls, and the honey-bees swarm around us. Aunt Fanny makes me eat a lot of truffles and a lot of cream buns on Sundays; if anything's left over, we take it to the Capuchin nuns. When it thunders, old Marie lies flat on her stomach under the kitchen table, and when it's fine we go and throw bundles of old letters, weighted with a big stone, into the river. Lots of people are doing the same thing. I enjoy myself very much.

Later, I come back to Riez with Uncle André and my cousins. It is raining. At the top of the hill we pass a little funeral procession, very small, all in black, which we can see from the coach. We arrive too late. Aunt Fanny has already gone. Old Marie is lying flat on her stomach under the table, crying. For the last time I pick some lilac. I do not see my little choirboy. I hum 'Come along, my chick' all alone. There are dead bees caught in my damp hair.

Meatball is my fiancé, big Urbain is my fiancé, the station-master is my fiancé, Albert, Jacques, Pierre, Grégoire, Philibert and all the others, all, all, are my fiancés. Carlotta, the cow in the meadow, with whom I play at christenings, Monsieur Martin's donkey, who comes to sleep in the greenhouse when I'm alone, and Milord, my old Milord, who is crippled with rheumatism, and who comes to have his back scratched. I chase the cat.

My first sorrow.

Meatball is going to the Sudan. He sends postcards and photographs of Negresses. I, too, buy a picture postcard: a handsome young man holding a bouquet of lilies of the valley. I send it to the Sudan. There! He's your rival, so you'd better be jealous, you naughty boy! And much, much later, when Meatball comes home, I shan't even spare him a glance. It's all over.

Marseille, Menton. I prefer my little garden.

Vichy. I have two embroidered dresses, one in Empire style. Heavens, how beautiful I look! But I still prefer the lilac at Riez.

The *lycée*. Grandmother takes me there. How boring it is! My only amusement is to go every day at five o'clock to see the mad people. My great friend, Madeleine, is the daughter of the director of the provincial asylum. We can go wherever we like. We can play in the courtyards, except in places where the walls are too close together. One day I climb into a fig tree to see what's behind the walls, and I fall and my hair gets caught in the branches and I hang there. How frightened I am! But afterwards, how we laugh! I could see the mad people on the other side of the wall. I spoke to them. If they say to you 'Good morning, cousin', you must answer 'Good morning, cousin'. And they are always talking about Lucie and Yvonne, who live with them all the time. Louise, the director's maid, who used to be a lunatic and is still a bit gaga, goes to fetch the eggs every day. She brings them into the house, but then she carries them back to the hen-house. How funny it is! A lot of the lunatics are very good gardeners.

I have taken my first communion. I am growing up. Every day I go to Aix for my piano lessons. Every day I take the train, and I am so pretty, so very pretty, that every day I have new sweethearts - sweethearts for five minutes, poor things! '. . . Mademoiselle! Mademoiselle!' They speak to me. I blush and blush, I am embarrassed, but very pleased. In the evening, on the train that is carrying me home, I talk about love. 'Today, my sweetheart is . . . is. . . .' Juliette and I nickname him Rosebud. Juliette is the new maid who takes me to school on the train. She is my only confidante. She is in love with the young chauffeur of the new doctor who has come to live in our neighbourhood. We call her sweetheart Snowflake, because of his white cap, and because he passes by so quickly. Mine is called Rosebud because he is so handsome.

Now we are always afraid of being late. We run all the way to the train, especially on the return journey, because it is only in the evenings that I can see Rosebud getting into the train. During the daytime he is already at the Faculty. He is studying law. He must come from Marseille because, when I get out, he stays on the train. We only travel together, on the same train, for a brief quarter of an hour. I lean just a little way out of the window. He is there. He is always there. He pretends to smoke a cigarette. He is in the carriage ahead of mine. What a thrill! Quick, quick, I must get out, we are there already! Juliette gives me a push. She bursts out laughing. My hat is all askew. My beautiful Sunday hat. A hat from Reboux. The train has already disappeared into the tunnel. There's nothing left but a cloud of smoke.

One day I travel alone. Rosebud, who always travels second class, leaves his compartment at Luynes and gets into my first-class carriage. We have just a few minutes, minus a tunnel, to look at each other. How eloquent his eyes are! I am very moved. In the tunnel I whisper his nickname: Rosebud, Rosebud.

'Juliette, my dear Juliette, tell me how babies are born. Through the stomach, isn't it? No? You don't want to tell me? If you don't tell me, I won't tell you that I saw Snowflake today! And he wasn't alone, your precious boy-friend!'

But Juliette won't say a word. She keeps all her secrets to herself.

. . . .

Cylinder Two (C)

Mireille's Little Exercise Book (continued)

. . . .

What has been happening lately?

The wind is blowing. It's winter. Papa is ill. The house is sad.

In the kitchen, Juliette and I still talk a bit about love. As Papa is laid up, I take advantage of it to go and read his books. I go into his surgery. I open a big medical tome. I read and read. I can't understand what it's about. One word has stuck in my head all through the winter, the word *emménagogue*. I don't quite know what it means. I just know it has something to do with the way babies are born. I found it in one of Papa's big books.

Papa is still ill. Mamma, who is so hale and hearty, cannot come. It is I who take care of Papa. Mamma is in Paris. She is working. From time to time she sends some money, which we send back to her. I am fed up. I can't bear it any longer. I think of Rosebud, who may be looking for me every evening on the train. I don't go to Aix any more. They've come to take away the piano Papa hired for me.

There has never been any money in the house. Papa was too good. He would never let people pay him. And now that he's ill, sick people no longer come to see him. Nobody ever comes to the house. Juliette, too, has left us to go into service with the new doctor. He has a motor car and his chauffeur, Snowflake, is Juliette's lover.

One day I go to Marseille without saying anything to Papa. I am afraid of meeting Rosebud there, because I am going to an antique shop to sell two old plates and make a little money. This is the first time I have ever been alone in a big city. I don't know anyone there except this antique dealer in the square in front of the Préfecture, where Grandmother took me once when she wanted to buy an old ivory crucifix. Grandmother died a long time ago. I wouldn't like to run into Rosebud. I wouldn't like him to know I'm short of money. Like a madwoman, I dash into the dealer's shop. Once, in front of Grandmother, this man patted my cheeks and said I was a dear, pretty little girl. I am in the antique shop. How can I tell him that I want to sell two old plates? How can I ask him for money? I am very scared. Someone strikes a Chinese gong behind me. How can I show him my plates? Every time a tram passes down the street, all the porcelain and crystal in the window shivers. The antique dealer is standing in front of me. He is very tall. He has a long black beard. I cannot speak. I make an effort. I start to cry. Suddenly the man takes me in his arms and kisses me on the lips. Ugh, how horrible! I drop my plates. I run out. Without even closing the door.

How horrible!

At home, Papa won't speak to me. We are angry with each other. How sad it is!

I really am all alone.

Juliette comes back, fat, fat, fat, and sad and silly. Why?

I have forgotten Rosebud.

It's all over now.

I have enough to worry about with Juliette, who is the laughing-stock of the whole neighbourhood. Everyone says she's going to have a baby. But I am convinced she's going to have typhoid. I should like to cut off her hair, like they do with typhoid patients.

Papa is better.

Soon he will be able to go out again.

He takes me to Marseille, to the cinema, the theatre. I don't find it at all amusing because Papa doesn't seem to enjoy anything any more. He doesn't sing now, he doesn't whistle. You'd think he would want to forget that he'd been ill. And we never hear anything from Mamma any more. How sad it is in the house! I would just as soon stay in the kitchen as go to the theatre in Marseille. Juliette and I spout mournful poetry to one another.

'L'Amour à Saint-Denis', such a beautiful poem, with a cynical refrain:

> She will abandon you
> Like those you've always seen
> Abandoning themselves to suffering
> When, suffering, one has abandoned them.
> Farewell!
> Never love!

My God, how melancholy we are!

Now we have lost everything, everything has been sold, the house, the garden, and all the rest. I do not know what has become of Juliette. They say she's had a baby, perhaps two at the same time, even three. People laugh at me in the street because I've always loved Juliette. Even Snowflake sticks out his tongue at me when he goes by.

Papa has given up everything. He has sold the gig he used on his rounds. He has even sold La Traviata, his old mare, the last offspring of Turco, the famous horse who was with him in the campaign of 1870.

Now, Papa takes me to Vichy in the summer and to Menton in the winter. The casino, the little horses, the balls, the great deserted hotels, the trains, the trunks . . . but I loved my little garden much better, with its Miranda jasmine and its sweet-scented stocks from Simiane, its patch of couch grass, its ants, its toad and its wild flowers, who all knew me.

One day, he took me to Paris. We could not visit Mamma. It seemed she was away on a trip, a business trip. I found Paris sad, the streets grey, with so many anxious-looking people everywhere. They all seemed to be in a hurry, and I think life there must be very hard. Only Papa was singing. He often took me to the rue Montorgueil. He was happy, it reminded him of his youth, when he was a student. We went on the omnibuses. 'You see there, on the corner? In my day, there was a man who sold watercress there. He used to sing "Watercress from the spring makes you healthy and strong!" And Papa began to sing in the street. And he also started humming a song he had known as a student, 'One day, a leopard . . .', as he used to when we made the rounds of his patients in the villages. One night, Papa stayed out all night. . . .

Just once more, I was to enjoy the high summer of my childhood freedom; after that, I was never again to return to Provence.

We spend the month of May at Eyrargues; a fortnight in La Crau; at harvest-time we are with Papa's cousins in Vaucluse; at Avignon we eat *fougassons*, dunking them in our *café au lait* in the mornings; at Châteauneuf-du-Pape I go on a grape cure; at Saint-Rémy-de-Provence Papa is treated for his rheumatism. My God, my God, I am a little girl again! My God, my God, how I should love to stay there, in my own home! At midnight, under the plane trees, we sing

'In the middle of my orchard . . .'

and in May, the month of Mary, there are the interminable processions, starting and ending at the church. How ardently Paul and Marguerite, some other little cousins and I speak the responses with the pious old ladies in the congregation. *Ora pro nobis*. We never leave out a single one. A hundred genuflexions. We make them all. And what sweet salutations in front of the shrines. Césarine, the big, dark-haired woman from the little farm, brings the *roses d'amour* to decorate the altar of the Virgin, and, in the early morning, if we can't go to pick the grapes because of the high winds, or if we have to wait a little while because there is too much dew on the vines, we girls amuse ourselves by tending the little secret garden, that little walled garden, full of nothing but roses, the *roses d'amour* that Césarine cultivates solely for the Virgin, and which we are forbidden to touch.

Papa is ill again. Mortally ill. This time it is serious. He has made his own diagnosis and, now that I am a very big girl, he says to me: 'My child, I have only four days left.'

As luck will have it, we are in a hotel room somewhere in a dreary provincial town where Papa had to stop because he felt too ill to go on.

Four days. During those four days I never leave his side. And when he starts to ramble, already delirious, I send telegrams to my mother, who is supposed to be in Paris, to my big brother, who works in a bank in Mexico, and to an older sister who is married and lives in Italy, although I've never seen her. Papa is delirious. How heart-breaking to see him like this! I can only sing as I choke back my tears:

> 'I have three jewels in a little casket.
>
> . . . .
> I have three jewels in a little casket.
>
> . . . .
> I have three jewels in a little casket'
>
> . . . .

There is nothing more I can say. Papa frightens me. He opens his eyes. It is the middle of the night. I am just tipping some ice into a bowl. Papa calls me. My heart stops beating. His eyes devour me.

'My child, my dear little girl,' he says, 'I must tell you my secret. This summer, at Vichy, I took three hundred francs out of your money-box.'

And he starts to cry.

I feel as if I am going to faint. I wish I could stop him talking.

'Climb up on the chair,' he says to me. 'There, on top of the wardrobe, in the lining of my bowler-hat, you will find a hundred francs. It's all that's left, all I can give you . . .'

I feel ice cold.

. . . .

The station-master has put Papa in the first-class waiting-room. I know all the local people in there. They are waiting for their families, who will arrive on the train from Paris. I am eaten up with misery, sitting in a big red plush armchair. I have brought Papa back home. On the wall there is an advertisement for the Paris–Marseille–Lyon line, which, at one time, tempted me to travel. . . . We are walking over crushed flowers. . . . At last Mamma has arrived, by the express. We spend the night with distant cousins. All night long I hear the tolling of the passing bell. It is 12th July. On the 13th I dress in black and dye my Italian straw hat with Indian ink. On 14th July I am in Paris. I am fifteen years old.

Mamma immediately takes me to the nuns on the rue Notre-Dame-des-Champs. Since then it has been raining non-stop. Since then the solitary chestnut tree in the courtyard has been shedding its leaves, which it does all the year round. Since then the sky has had a rusty look. Since then Mamma has come to visit me on only one Thursday in every month. She takes me out for a walk in the Luxembourg Gardens, which are full of wounded men. We go to drink hot chocolate, then I come back. I do not know anything. I do not know how to pray. I hear the whisperings in the long corridors of this old convent, the clicking of rosaries and, sometimes, coming from the cellars, a sound like a train passing in the distance. They say France is at war. There is a crucifix on the wall. I am cold. Sometimes, the whole house shakes. I am all alone in my long night-dress. I crumple a piece of paper that is lying over my heart. It is Papa's last hundred francs.

Cylinder Three

. . . .

The night is blue.

I cannot sleep.

I am looking out of the window.

The night grows bluer and bluer.

It is dawn. Or almost.

During February it rained. Now the föhn, the great storm-wind has dropped. The winter is starting again. It's snowing.

The night is blue.

During February it rained. During the whole of the month of February I dictated Mireille's little exercise book into the machine. Avalanches rolled down the valley. The first broke off from the Brévent. I had a very good view of it. Another one, at Bel-Achat, cut the railway line to Les Gaillants. One day I went as far as Pierre Pointue. The Taconnaz and Les Bossons glacier were fuming. La Jonction was full of thunder. Facing me, the Mont des Corbeaux was all muffled up in dirty clouds, and the clouds were pissing into the valley. The fog reached up to the *Plan*, to the level of my door. All around I heard water trickling in the valley, water and furious gusts of wind. But at night it froze hard. During the night, rocks split off from the flanks of the Aiguille.

At night I listened to all these sounds.

As soon as it calmed down, I went down to Chamonix, but I

always came back up from there as soon as I'd had enough, whatever the weather, even if the storm was raging, even if it was dark. I went down half a dozen times. Maybe more. I know perfectly well that the guides say I'm mad and tell all sorts of stories about me in the inns. They point their fingers at me as I pass. 'There's that lunatic!' They are convinced I'm going to kill myself. But I love to battle with the elements, the storm, the night; I am not afraid of them, nor of the hard climb up, in winter, via Les Tissours and the *chalet du Trois*. It reminds me of the finest time of my life, at Balleny and at Port Deception when . . . but I know that I shall never again surprise the whales when they're mating. Ah, what a spectacle!

The end of the season. They're closing up. There's nobody left in Chamonix. It's over. The last direct train with a drawing-room car has gone. The bob-sleigh runs are deserted. Winter sports are over, so there are no more crowds on the skating-rink, no more streamers, no more voices, no more of those ringing shouts I could hear right up on the *Plan*, no more brass bands. Perhaps it was this sudden gap in my life, made by the departure of the crowds and the musicians, that drove me to leave the chalet and go down to the town so often. Thank you, then, thank you to the fashionable set, and to the sportsmen, now that they've gone.

The Majestic is deserted. They're battening down the hatches. They're putting dust-sheets over the furniture in the lounges, and the thousand bedrooms are being locked up one by one. Each day the shutters on another floor are nailed up. There are mountains of mattresses in the corridors and it is only as a special favour that, for a little while longer, they are letting me keep on the suite on the corner of the first floor which serves me as a *pied-à-terre* when I go down to the town. But I know quite well I am a nuisance. The domestic staff are leaving too. I run into them round about the station. They are waiting for their trains. Meanwhile they drink white wine in the inns. On the pavement in front of every café you see old, battered, bulging, unmatched suitcases with the old labels half peeled off. They are getting wet. Now that the last luxury train has left, the trains that arrive every day are stormed by chambermaids in hats, and floor waiters whom I no longer recognize because now they address me as *tu* and offer me drinks.

The porter still comes, every morning, to smoke his pipe in the last remaining armchair in the lobby. When the weather clears, he trains the hotel telescope on Mont Blanc. He no longer has to put a sou in the slot on the machine - now that there are no more clients, it's free. Every time I arrive, he calls me and shows me the smoke coming out of my chalet chimney. I have a fire burning up there.

'So, you've come down again, eh, Monsieur Jacques? You get bored all on your own. But there's nobody left here. We're closing up.'

The porter is not in uniform and he no longer bothers to shave. He smokes an old, well-seasoned pipe. I ask him for a light. He always calls me Monsieur Jacques, because he thinks that's my name. Like a true Swiss, he has never been able to pronounce 'Dan Yack'.

They're closing up. It's raining. They're closing up. Everything is sopping wet. Pedestrians splash through the muddy snow, and the iron runners on the sledges often grind against the cobblestones. As always happens at the end of the season, there are a few loiterers. This year they are three women who have been unable to pay their accounts at the hotel. The management of the Majestic has driven them out and settled them in the little Hotel Payot. I often go there. By an odd coincidence, all three women are called Bella. The Baroness Bella Przybiszuilska; Bella Pharaon, an adventuress from London, who is waiting for her monthly remittance to pay her bill and flit; Bella Fridricks, a pretty little pink piglet. I have slept with all three Bellas by way of doing them a favour and enabling them to leave. (Bella Fridricks told me her car had been stolen.) But what draws me to the little Hotel Payot is a waitress, whose name is not Bella but Lucienne, Lucie, Lucia, Luce, Lucette, Suzette, Lulu or Zézette. She is as beautiful as she is stupid. She doesn't want to come to Paris with me. She says I frighten her. I wonder why? She says I'm too rich and that she can't understand why I've spent the winter all alone up in the mountains. Perhaps she's right, because she comes from Saint-Nicolas-de-Véroce and she knows the mountains well. Anyway I shall go and see her in her village this summer, in the country. Lucienne works only in the winter; in the summer, she stays at home to help with the haymaking. She has three brothers, one of whom is a soldier. She gives herself to me very tenderly, but she is always a bit afraid and won't accept any kind of present. Nothing. Like the porter at the Majestic, she calls me Monsieur Jacques. She's never managed to pronounce Yack, Dan Yack. When she tried, it made her laugh. At night she purrs, softly and very sweetly.

The night is blue.

The night is blue.

The night is blue.

Lucienne has gone, too. I didn't need my field-glasses to see her go by. At my feet, two thousand metres down, she waved her handkerchief from the train, as I had told her to. And I fired my rifle. Two shots.

It's well and truly over.

The night is blue.

The night is blue, like it is in Paris.

It is dawn. Or almost.

In the past, I used to go on the binge in Paris.

The night is blue, like it is when you come out of some shady dive and walk down from Montmartre at dawn.

The night is blue.

How many times have I seen the night grow blue, through the door of a bar or the open window of a brothel, on the place des Victoires!

It was during the war.

Every time, I had a fight with Théréson over that open window. Théréson claimed that I would get her fined and have the neighbours up in arms against her. In Paris, the windows had to be shut because of the Zeppelins. Neither Théréson, nor her clients, nor her girls, not even the Negress, were afraid of the Zeppelins and nobody ever bothered to go down to the cellars when the air-raid warning sounded. But Théréson was stubborn. She didn't want any trouble and I must close my window. It was no use showing her my car out in the square, with its General Staff flag, since Théréson was not afraid of the police (she paid for her licence) but of her neighbours, owing to all the rumours about spies.

Ah! That car! It was a big Studebaker. One night I went upstairs without even turning off the engine, I was in such a hurry to see my good Théréson, the Madame, who purred (like the more recent Lucienne) as she took me into her arms and scratched my back with her ring finger, something Lucienne had never learned to do; Théréson scratched my back, right between the shoulder-blades, for hours and hours, as we made, unmade and remade love.

I remember that famous night – oh yes, I remember it! I remember it because of the car, because of Théréson, because of the open window, because of our squabble, because of the police who were down in the square, standing round my car and refusing to budge as long as the engine was running, because of Théréson, who wanted to go down in her night-dress and turn it off, because of myself, I, who didn't want to go down and lay on the bed rocking with laughter at the sight of Théréson going off her head with indignation, because of the house that was in an uproar over the engine, which was turning ever more slowly, because of the good friends who had come with me and were now laughing at me, at Théréson, at the police, at the engine, and who were yelling jokes at me through the partition walls, and because of the day that was to follow.

It was raining.

Through the open window, the night was blue.

The night was blue.

By the time the engine stopped, out of petrol, it was dawn.

A blue dawn.

It was 11th November 1918.

Armistice Day.

How could I forget that day! Paris was in a delirium. Midday. Théréson and the girls go out. Guns roar. I fill up the car. I load everybody into my General Staff car. We tour the *grands boulevards*. We sing, we shout, we yell. The crowd cheers us, my friends and me. Each of us buys a case of champagne. We buy armfuls of flags. And, all of a sudden, Théréson decides to go and see her daughter, who is in a convent. We all go along, too. She throws herself into her daughter's arms, crying: 'Ah! What a day! Ah! My poor little girl! If only your father were here!'

Théréson sobbed.

The young girl looked at us, dumbfounded. My comrades became serious. The women arranged their hair. I straightened my uniform. The little girl stared at us, one after the other. I saw her go pale, bite her lips, bat her eyelids. I expected to see her burst into tears but, instead, she flung her arms round my neck and began to laugh and laugh.

'Let's go, Théréson, let's go!'

I bundled everybody into the car. We set off. The young girl was sitting beside me. I was at the steering-wheel.

It was Mireille.

. . . .

From the Pont du Gard to la Durance,
From Barbentane to Tarascon,
Of all the girls in old Provence,
The fairest one was Théréson.
She could not speak a word except:
            Quès aco?

        Digo li qué vengué,
        Mon bon!

. . . .

Yes. Théréson Chastelas is Mireille's mother. How can I explain it? She had never spoken to me about her daughter. And at last, here she was!

Mireille was sitting beside me, almost on my knees, as I drove. Théréson was on her other side. She was still crying. I drove very slowly because of the crowds in the streets. In the rear mirror I could see Merle of Agen kissing the Jewess smack on the lips. There were two other women in the car with my comrades-in-arms, Taylor and Brown. They were singing and shouting. They acknowledged the ovations of the crowd, who were cheering us with *Vive les Anzacs!* People climbed on to the running-boards, they clung to the wings. We advanced in fits and starts. Everybody was milling about, it was crazy. What gaiety! What singing! Ah, those old choruses! All these men and women were delirious with joy. Paris was magnificent. In the place de la Concorde an

American sailor sat himself astride the bonnet and unfurled an enormous Stars and Stripes. Long ago someone had swiped my little General Staff flag. In front of the Marivaux Cinema a bareheaded woman got into the car and kissed me passionately on the lips. She did it a dozen times. Then she jumped out, snatched off my cap, and shouted to Mireille, as she spun round and did a few waltz-steps: 'Hey, kid! I've had your handsome officer, y'know? You're a lucky girl, you are!'

Paris was magnificent. Parades marched past, we crossed them, we led them, we followed them. For hours we parked beneath the windows of clubs and newspapers. We threw flowers, as if we were on the Corso, or at the Carnival in Nice. People were hoarse from so much singing, always the same refrain:

> Here comes our soldier-boy,
> Tra-la-la-la-lah!
> Here comes our soldier-boy
> Back from the war!

or

> Ah, he never should have gone,
> No, he never should have gone there, anyway!

They had hooked a 77* on to the back of my car, and I hadn't even noticed. Mireille murmured in my ear: 'So, my friend, you're Australian?'

'No, no, Mademoiselle, I'm English.'

'Ah!'

She went on: 'And you've come from a long way away?'

'From the other side of the world.'

'Ah!'

'I couldn't explain to you where, it's too far.'

'And did you come to fight for France?'

'Yes, Mademoiselle, I came to fight.'

'My poor friend! And did you kill many of the enemy?'

---

* A 77-millimetre gun, though this was a German not an Allied weapon. Possibly Cendrars had in mind a captured war trophy.

'Yes, Mademoiselle, a great many.'

'My poor friend!' Mireille repeated tenderly.

I told her how I had killed twenty-eight Boches one day, before breakfast, just for fun, like shooting pigeons in Monte Carlo.

'Oh my dear, I feel so frightened for you!' murmured Mireille, squeezing my arm.

She was thoughtful.

I observed her out of the corner of my eye.

My God! How beautiful she was!

Mireille went on: 'Tell me, the war is horrible, isn't it?'

'No, why?'

'I don't know why, but all those horrors . . .'

'Well, you know, Mademoiselle, I've seen a good many of those, and not just in the war . . .'

'Ah! And what did you do before the war?'

'I was a whale-hunter, Mademoiselle.'

And I started telling her about my hunting, about my life down there at Port Deception, how we used to set off in a little boat armed with a harpoon-gun and surprise the whales, which very often travelled in couples, or perhaps it would be a mother with her young one. First, you harpoon the whale-calf, then the mother exposes herself to all your shots. When she is mortally wounded, she sweats with anguish, she foams, she sweats blood. That's what we call making her 'flower'. I also told her about my wanderings, when I would go off alone and shoot seals, and about my long rambles amongst the penguin rookeries. Flocks of penguins look like flocks of nuns. They are black and white. The little ones are yellow like chicks, but they soon turn brown. They have eyes like big black boot-buttons. There is no creature so absurd, so comical, so droll and so sensible. Penguins go fishing in the early morning and sometimes travel long distances. They cross the ice-fields by gliding along on their bellies. They make a lot of fuss before they dive in, encouraging each other, pushing and shoving one another. On their return, they escort or carry the injured and the sick ones, and at night they post sentinels at each of the four corners of their camp. These sentinels bray like donkeys. They cry out and answer each other every quarter of an hour. Their cry sounds like a badly played trumpet; it's also

39

like the cry of a peacock, but hollower, not so sharp. It's a bit husky. When you walk among their nests, the penguins swear at you. They look at you dumbfounded, they flap their wings, peck at your boots, shit copiously, insult you, fall silent, gaze at you. They smell terrible. They collect stones.

'Oh, my dear friend, I love you,' Mireille said to me, pressing herself close to me, so that I felt the full weight of her body.

'Me, too, I . . .'

'My dear friend, I've been waiting for you for such a long time!'

'Me too!'

I was so excited that I underlined this confession by cutting out the exhaust.

It was getting dark.

Around us the fairy lights, the garlands of light, the chandeliers were being lit on all the balconies. Far from thinning out or moving away, the crowds grew ever denser. We couldn't move any more. We were somewhere behind the Madeleine. So, abandoning the car, I led the whole party into the little *Tabac* on the rue Tronchet. We had a hard time getting through the crowd.

In the *Tabac* things were jumping. We crunched over oyster-shells and broken glasses, waded through confetti, got our feet tangled in the paper streamers which were strewn all over the floor, paddled through puddles of spilled wine, trampled flowers, kicked up the sawdust. People were coming in from the street through the open windows, with flags, songs, bombs and firecrackers, and taking the tables by storm. The men were in shirt-sleeves and the women were drunk from exhaustion, excitement and champagne. Everybody was hoarse, they'd lost their voices, but they kept on singing all the same. Big Marcelle, the *patronne*, a capable women who had a soft spot for me - she used to sell me contraband cigars and cook special dishes for me - led us up to the mezzanine floor. She opened her bedroom for us, and it was there we sat down to table. The whole bunch were dying of hunger. Except me.

I had no desire to eat now.

Why?

Because.

Because before we sat down to table, Théréson had disappeared.

And, before disappearing, she had beckoned me to follow her. As the lavatory was occupied, we went into the kitchen. And it was there, in a narrow passageway between steaming saucepans and spitting frying-pans, where we were deafened by shouted orders, jostled and shoved by waiters and waitresses, and watched by the mocking eyes of Big Marcelle, who was preparing lobster *à l'américaine* especially for us, that Théréson once more burst into tears and I had to calm her down.

She wept on my breast, amongst my medals.

'My dear, she loves you! What will become of me? What can I do?' She was frantic.

'What can I do about my daughter, now that she knows everything? I can't send her back to the nuns. It's much too late, and besides, besides, I have my house to run. I can't stay away on a night like this!'

She was in a fearful tizzy.

'Listen, Théréson, listen to me. Don't get upset,' I said to her, 'I give you my word of honour . . .'

'And Mireille, she knows everything! I never wanted her to find out, never . . . I never wanted her to know that her mother . . . is . . . is . . . a . . .'

'Théréson! I assure you Mireille hasn't noticed a thing. Leave it to me. I swear to you . . .'

'Mireille! She's a shrewd girl! Ah, my husband, my poor husband! An old soldier! On a day like this! And I've done everything to . . .'

'Calm yourself, Théréson! Listen, you go back, very quietly, without saying a word to anyone. Do you trust me? I . . .'

'Trust you? Yes, but only you! Help me, I beg you! I would die of shame if. . . . Take her away, hide her, don't ever let her see me again!'

'Right! You slip away. I'll go back upstairs. We'll have dinner. Then I'll take Mireille away. She won't suspect a thing. I'll rent a suite at the Ritz. Don't worry, I'll take good care of her. Put your mind at rest. You trust me, don't you? She can stay at the Ritz till I come back, because I've got to rejoin my regiment, you know. Afterwards, afterwards, I'll explain everything to her. I . . . I . . . Théréson, I am asking for your daughter's hand.

Madame Chastelas, will you give me your daughter in marriage?'

'No! You're not serious!'

'I'm serious, you know I am.'

'And what are you going to say to her?'

'We'll see . . . we'll see . . . I . . . I . . . I'll tell her . . . that . . . I . . .'

'Come, let me embrace you, you are the dearest and best of men!'

Théréson hugged me.

Everything was spinning around me.

There was a frightful racket coming from the café.

Guns were being trundled along the street, pulled by students and schoolboys. Little shop-girls, street urchins, old folk, war wounded, a blind man, everybody was yoked to the guns. They were beating out the rhythm of the 'Marseillaise' on plates, on glasses. Soldiers on leave were whistling into the necks of empty bottles. Chairs, tables were sagging under the weight of all the people climbing on to them to watch the parades in the street. At one moment we were almost separated by a parade of madmen who came right into the kitchen, bawling and shouting, banging on the saucepan lids, upsetting stacks of dishes.

'I give her to you,' Théréson breathed into my ear, 'I give her to you, my dearest!'

I pushed her gently towards the counter and poured her a drink. Théréson recovered her spirits a little. She was no longer a weeping mother, but a woman in love, stammering incoherent phrases.

'You're a good sort, really, a good sort. . . . What an idea! . . . With you, one has to be prepared for anything. . . . Nobody else would have thought of such a thing. . . . What a surprise! And to think you're serious about it . . . you, you . . . you who make a joke of everything . . . I know she'll be happy with you. . . . And Mireille will never know, never know anything?'

'I swear to you, Théréson.'

'Ah!'

Before disappearing into the crowd, she had one last scruple: 'And you think Mireille will accept you?'

'I don't know . . . I . . .'

'And what will you say to her?'
'I'll phone you later.'

. . . .

I rang up. But, before that, I had gone back up to the mezzanine floor to fetch Mireille.

We went out into the street.

We were laughing like a couple of kids.

Paris was magnificent.

Ah! That night.

. . . .

Cylinder Four

At the Chalet, 17th March

The night is blue. During the day, I talk into my machine. At night, I go out.

I do not sleep.

For a fortnight now, the nights have been blue, a quite extraordinary blue. For a fortnight the weather has been fine. For a fortnight it has been freezing. It is winter. The real thing. Naturally the sports lovers have not come back, and yet this is just the moment when it would be good to go tobogganing. In February, when it was raining, they were still holding skiing contests in the valley. Why? All the hotels are closed. Chamonix is empty, deserted. Even the local inhabitants stay shut up in their houses. They're probably asleep. Today they are a degenerate race. On these beautiful sunny days, and on these beautiful nights, so cold, so celestially cold, I never see a soul in the valley. There's never anyone on the roads, even when I look through my field-glasses. I can't hear a sound. Even when I hang right out and look down into the valley, there's nothing moving. I think even the trains have stopped running. I smoke my pipe. Not a bird in sight. Not a cry.

Nobody comes.

Only once, throughout the whole winter, have I had a visitor here.

Naturally he was an Englishman.

A few days after New Year I saw a party of three, roped together, coming up. I burst out laughing when I saw them. It was so unexpected! And there they were, stopping on the terreplein in front of my door. The Englishman saluted me, raising his hand to his camel-hair Balaclava. As for me, I burst out laughing again, for I was bareheaded. Naturally we did not speak to each other. The Englishman sent me his guide as a go-between. It was the Giant, a great-great-nephew of the great Jacques Balmat, known as Mont Blanc, that famous man who was lost in these mountains looking for gold among the glaciers.

The great Balmat was not mad. I have seen little grains of gold collected from the springs of the Diosaz and I have heard that it was in those parts – but on the other side of the mountain, on the Ruan glacier – that Jacques Balmat disappeared. Besides, what matters is not the gold but Balmat's prune-stones.

The guides and porters have often told me this story.

The great Balmat was the first to reach the summit of Mont Blanc, and he did it alone. Now it seems that, at the time, he had three prunes in his pocket, so he buried them in the snow at the summit as a testimony to his exploit. All the guides who reached the peak later on looked for these three prunes, but not one of them had the luck to lay hands on them. More than a hundred years later, when they were digging through the ice-cap at the summit to get down to the rock and build solid foundations for the Janssen Observatory, they found, about forty metres down, the stones of three prunes. There was no doubt about it, they were Balmat's prunes. This discovery immediately provoked violent battles amongst the men working there. Everyone wanted to appropriate these relics, to which the mountaineers attributed talismanic virtues of protection and good luck. As a result, every hamlet in the valley was on the war-path. There were fierce vendettas, hatred between clans, brother turning against brother, complicated crimes, bizarre accidents on the mountain, chalets burned down, in this secret battle for possession of the three prune-stones. The first man to own them was François Coutet, killed at Sixt while stalking chamois. Between then and 1914 – that is to say, in less than twenty years – there were the following

45

deaths: the three Dévouassou brothers, who perished together at Mont Maudit; Lombard, known as Jorasse, who was found hanged in the chapel at Les Tines; one of the Cachats, killed on the mountain; one of the Tourniers, killed on the mountain; a certain François Ravenet, who disappeared in a crevasse. The guides and porters, who are all superstitious men, lay the blame for these 'misfortunes' at the door of science and that damned scientist who went and set up an observatory on Mont Blanc. Certainly Janssen left a very bad reputation behind him in these parts. I've seen women cross themselves at the mention of his name. When they talk about him, the locals still call him 'The Devil'. The last case was, again, a Coutet, Marie Coutet, who possessed these famous prune-stones. He had had them since 1914. He showed them to me when he sublet the chalet on the *Plan* to me for the winter. He always carried them in his waistcoat pocket. He's a distrustful man, a grimacing savage, the only guide without a licence, but he knows the mountain like the back of his hand. Everyone's afraid of him. I suspect that, when he says he's looking for crystals, he's really looking for gold, like the great Balmat. The others spy on him. One day he led me up to the summit of the Aiguille du Plan by climbing up the passoir de l'Aiguille, against the south-west face, which is sheer and has always been considered unscalable.

I was interested in the construction of the observatory on Mont Blanc because of the factory I had had built at Port Deception, amongst the Antarctic ice, and I liked getting Marie Coutet to talk about 'The Devil'. Coutet knew him well, because it was he who was unanimously delegated to carry the heavy lens of the telescope up to the summit. They reckoned it would kill him. Although it was extremely fragile, the lens weighed ninety kilos, and it was a load that couldn't be shared. Marie Coutet agreed to do it. But imagine his amazement when, after loading the lens on to his grappling-irons, and his grappling-irons on to his back, he saw Jenssen coming towards him, armed with a long steel chain. This puny little runt of a man came hopping along on one foot, knotted the chain around Coutet's waist and bound it round him – him, Marie Coutet, the strongest and most fiercely independent of all the mountaineers! He passed the chain under his arms, crossed it over his chest, wound it ten times round his precious lens, knotted it over the hooks, passed it once more over his shoulders and, in short, bound the porter to his load and tied him up like a parcel. Finally, Janssen turned the key in the padlock.

Knowing the man, I can easily imagine how furious, how indignant Marie Coutet was.

Nevertheless, he was the first to set off.

What consoled him was the thought that his comrades had come off no better than he had. In fact, Janssen had little confidence in his men. They were all chained and padlocked to their loads, for fear they would jettison their precious cargo if they got into difficulties. Janssen himself, who was disabled – I've never been able to make out whether he was really a cripple, bandy-legged, twisted, stricken with Pott's disease or simply a dwarf – installed himself in a sort of sledge-cum-armchair-cum-sedan-chair of his own invention, and had himself hoisted, carried and hauled up to the summit. The crew who manhandled this vehicle were the most tightly chained of the lot: to add insult to injury, Janssen swore at them every inch of the way. He was a wretched, nasty little toad. Everyone detested him.

All went well as far as the pierre à l'Echelle, but when it came to roping up, nobody would agree to run the risk of having Marie Coutet in his party. He was too heavily laden. He might take a false step. It was too dangerous. So, he set out all alone, boldly, at the head of the whole party.

He crossed the crests. In the crevasses he let himself slither forward on his belly so as not to damage his load. It was a point of honour with him to deposit his load, intact, at the summit. He swore, he cursed, he laboured and sweated, he wished life, mankind and the mountain would go to the devil, but still he kept on climbing. He wanted to get there first. When he couldn't carry on, he let himself fall full length, buried his head in the snow and breathed like a bear. A hundred times he thought he was about to die, he had the sensation that his heart, his whole being, was going to burst; a hundred times he overcame these moments of weakness. He didn't want to stop at the Grands Mulets. He camped for the night on the Plateau, at the foot of the Rochers Rouges, still chained to his load. All alone. He confessed to me that, when he was crossing the long ridge of the Dromedaire next day, which looks like a double snow-roof, he felt like throwing himself into the void, lens and all, for he felt such hatred for this astronomer who had no confidence in his men, such hatred for his companions, such hatred for himself. When he reached the summit, he didn't know how to give vent to his rage and contempt, so he used his ice-axe to cut the word SHIT in gigantic letters in the frozen snow. Then he fell on his knees and passed out.

Marie Coutet would never accept payment for that climb, but he swore to get his revenge.

That's the kind of man he was.

I think he kept his word by finally becoming master of Balmat's three prune-stones.

Less than three weeks ago he was found crushed beneath a pine-tree he had just cut down. It was alleged to be an accident. Nobody knows what has become of the three prune-stones. His waistcoat pocket was empty. . . .

Well then, the Giant came, on behalf of his Englishman, to propose that I should accompany them to Mont Blanc.

'Tell the gentleman', I said to the Giant, 'that I've just come down.'

'What, today?'

'Yes, exactly, I've just got back.'

'All alone?'

'All alone.'

'But you're mad!'

'So they tell me, Giant. But now clear off, I've seen quite enough of you.'

I can still see them decamping, and I laugh out loud in front of my dictaphone, as I laughed on that day.

.   .   .   .

I do not sleep. So at night I go out. In the daytime I speak into my machine. But at night I go out, like a thief.

What long rambles!

The full moon is immense.

Everything is transparent.

I walk, my pipe clamped in my muzzle, an iron-tipped stick in my hand. Nothing disturbs my thoughts, not even the distant barking of a dog. I can't stand dogs any more, that's why I don't have one here. I don't want any more dogs.

I am alone.

I cross the lake of the *Plan*, covered at this season with enormous chunks of debris that have fallen from the Aiguille. I go as far as Blaitières-dessus, or else I push on as far as the moraine of Les Nantillons. There is a ledge of rock there which hangs out over the void. I often sit there. Smoking.

Nothing disturbs my thoughts. Nothing distracts me. The springs, the torrents, the waterfalls, the cascades of water are all frozen.

I am all alone.

I stand up to roll a lump of rock off the moraine. I choose a lump of granite, almost cube-shaped, and, using my stick as a lever, I manage to start it moving. At first the block slides slowly on the ice, then it crashes on to its anterior face. It rocks for a moment, then begins to roll. It seems to gather momentum, the slope becomes steeper, it makes a huge bound and disappears into the void. I follow its fall, watching the splinters fly and listening to the shattering of tumbling rocks. All that lot will go down and crush the forest of the Planaz. Down below. More than a thousand metres down.

When all is silent again, I go back to my observation post. I listen. I smoke. Nothing disturbs my thoughts.

Everything is blue. The frowning crests. The ice. The full moon. The sky. The night. Ah, the night!

This is the hour when the stars palpitate.

This is the hour when, in Paris, you hear the horses' hoofs on the wooden cobbles. The first delivery vans are already coming back from Les Halles. There is a clatter of milk bottles, announcing the approach of dawn. A little later a cyclist goes by, whistling. I am at my window overlooking the place Vendôme. I am in my pyjamas, smoking a cigarette. I have already had my bath. I have not been to bed, because by now I have ceased to sleep. I have perfumed myself with vetiver. The dawn chill gives me goose-pimples. Outside, everything is becoming an intense blue. At the Ritz, too, my room was blue.

49

I lean out. Down below, the night porter is handing over to the day porter. I can hear them laughing. The valets are beating carpets. The municipal water-carts are circling round the column like insects on a pond. The first newspapers are being delivered. In the room next door Mireille is asleep in a big bed. The canopy over her head is also blue.

She is there.

We are married.

But before?

Before, I came back from the war. Before, I was demobilized. Before, I was put under arrest because of that car I had lost on the night all Paris was celebrating the Armistice. Before, I had telephoned Théréson. I had told her: 'Yes, Mireille is very happy about it.'

Before, it was wine, women and high old times. Before, it was the war. Wartime nights. Bapaume, the Somme, the Battle of Saint-Quentin, Cow Wood. Before. . . .

It is dawn.

I come back to the chalet.

I take a stiff drink and start speaking into the machine again.

I no longer sleep at all.

My insomnia.

It took the war to change my life.

No, it took the war to reveal me as I really was, as I had always been – that is, innocent and full of childishness.

I like to enjoy myself.

At Port Deception I had embarked on a venture from which I could not escape. I was beginning to get bored. I was demoralized. I didn't even have the courage to leave. It took the war to . . .

Ah, Mireille!

Before, before . . . oh well, never mind!

. . . .

Then, as now, winter was drawing to a close. Out at sea, the spring thaw had already taken place. It was, I believe, the eighth or ninth year that I'd been there. I was ready to abandon the whole enterprise, to hand it all over to Hortalez and make him, quite simply, a present of the Sociedad Ballenera Chilotes, my whaling company. I wanted to leave and never to hear his name again – nor the name of Doña Heloisa. I'd had enough.

One day the arrival of the whaling fleet was signalled. It was coming in much earlier than usual. The smoke from innumerable smoke-stacks, some of them huge, announced its approach. In Community City excitement ran high. The first to set foot on dry land was Dr Schmoll, who disembarked from a dinghy flying the ensign of the German navy. Nobody understood the significance of this display. On the contrary, I was very happy to see our doctor back again, for I had dreamed up an idea for a giant gramophone with a needle as big as a coach-bolt. I was counting on Schmoll to construct this magnificent machine, which I planned to set up in the main square of Community City, like a bandstand. I wanted to present it to my men as a final surprise before I departed. I would not leave without fulfilling this vow. I also wanted to ask the doctor whether it would be possible to extract a material similar to ebonite, for the manufacture of gramophone records, from the residue of our whales. I dreamed of records as big as a ballroom floor.

Two hundred and seventy-five boats, thirty-seven of them large colliers, had dropped anchor in our port. Like Schmoll's dinghy, they had all hoisted their colours. Guns were trained on the town. And, although only a few of the men who disembarked were in uniform, every one of them was armed.

As I said, nobody realized the significance of this demonstration, and it was quite pointless for Schmoll to threaten me with a big revolver as I went to greet him. To deploy all these armed forces here was ridiculous in the extreme. Personally, I saw nothing more in the whole business than an unlooked-for opportunity to change my life.

When Schmoll announced that he was taking possession of the island and, consequently, of my whaling enterprise, the flensing-station and the town, and that all my ships were being commandeered, I burst out laughing in his face. It seemed I was a ruined man. What a bit of luck!

The Germans' first task was to install a radio station on the island and to set up a battery of two guns at the entry to the fairway. They disembarked tons of equipment. The radio station and its antennae were rapidly erected. The Germans listened in constantly. It seemed they kept in continuous communication with the Falklands and jammed all the messages coming out of that station. They also broadcast false signals, with the ships' call-signs, so that they could not be located and charted. When the men emerged from the radio station, they were always excited and laughing amongst themselves. I took no notice of them; for myself, I had no complaint against them. As far as I was concerned, I had to put up with a gang of pirates, superbly organized, it is true – and this surprised me rather, as did the authority that Schmoll seemed to wield over them, the discipline he imposed and the prestige he enjoyed. Schmoll appeared to be in expectation of grave events, but, as nothing ever happened, the Germans themselves began whale-catching and settling in for a long sojourn, for, in this kind of climate, one must always be prepared for an enforced overwintering. The whaling flourished as never before. It was a weird summer.

At Port Deception the catches had always been good. The rorquals were plentiful. There were enormous pods of them. Sometimes there were right whales, especially females with their little ones, who came from the seas around the Cape, where they liked to remain during gestation. In spite of this, it was not unusual to see the whaling fleets steaming far to the south. In the preceding year I had even sent a factory ship to anchor at Port Charcot, beyond Graham Land. This year the catch took place in the waters of Port Deception itself, never out of sight of the island. That was as far as anyone could go. *Primo*, because the Germans wouldn't have allowed anyone out, and, *secundo*, because the fast-ice surrounded and enclosed us very tightly.

It was a weird summer, not blue, but red, bright red. Everybody was red with blood.

After an early spell of good weather and a rapid thaw, which had permitted the inopportune arrival of Schmoll's fleet, the cold had launched a second, vigorous offensive. The pack-ice had re-formed. The bay-ice besieged us. There was barely one channel of open water, a ragged semicircle with a sinuous branch extending out towards the west. It seemed as if every whale in the Antarctic Ocean had made a rendezvous in this pocket of water. The men set to with a will.

What a massacre! The whales abounded. They were so

numerous that we had no time to aim harpoons at them, we simply rammed them. The boats drove full steam ahead into them. From the blow-hole there would be a sudden spout of blood instead of a column of water. Hurrah! Hurrah! In a matter of seconds the men's arms, their hands, their faces were as red as their red woollen shirts.

It was nothing but men yelling, whistles blowing, shouted orders, improvised manoeuvres, mad dashes, the death-flurry of whales, giant cadavers stranded on the coastal pack-ice or tossed in the heavy swell as they were towed alongside. Thousands of sea-birds swooped down on our victims, disputing their rights with us even on the flensing-plan. What carnage! The men were drunk with blood, overwork, joy. They did a magnificent job. I worked with them.

I had drawn an unlucky number. I was working on board whale-catcher number 116, which had a German crew; they were novices and their clumsiness very nearly caused several accidents. In spite of that, I retain happy memories of those days. Those few months of intensive manual work, brutalizing and back-breaking, of over-exertion, fatigue and risks that I shared with my men certainly formed part of the finest epoch of my life.

Have you never felt that you wanted to walk up the ramp, get up there on the stage, or enter the circus arena, or roll up your sleeves and grab a tool when you've stopped in front of a building-site to watch others work? As for me, I like to put my hand to the job. There is so much joy in action. I can't restrain myself. It doesn't much matter what one does. I know how to drive a locomotive and I have been underwater in a diver's suit. What hard work! Your mind is empty. You have to know how to breathe inside the helmet in counterpoint to the rhythm of the pump that is supplying you with fresh air. And then you are never heavy enough. There is always the tendency to rise up. It is weird. Divers get good wages. They are silent types. They eat and drink heartily.

On board whale-catcher 116 I had become an expert in handling the lance. It takes a lot of strength, and still more skill, to strike the whale precisely in the hollow of the left axilla, where the pads of fat are not so thick, and ram the lance in with a single thrust, deep into the thoracic cage. If you hit the bone, the instrument

53

glances off the shoulder-blade and you run the risk of falling into the water. On one occasion we were lashed to a large ice-floe. I had gone down in the longboat to drive the lance into a whale that was about to sink. It was an arduous operation. The whale was in an awkward position. A cable had been passed under its belly and they were manoeuvring it from the ship, at the capstan, trying to pivot it towards me. I was just gathering momentum to aim and drive in the lance when the boat struck against the ice-floe and the cable of the windlass broke. One end of the cable snapped back on me like a spring, wound itself round my neck and threw me up in a high trajectory. That day I narrowly escaped being strangled, drowned, decapitated and hanged. I still have a long scar behind my ear.

So, I lived the life of my men, that punch-drunk life in which you eat and sleep when you can, work yourself to death, and drink plenty of booze so as not to feel how your strength is ebbing away, you spend every last ounce of your energy, and you become so brutalized that you are no longer capable of thought. I was no longer thinking about anything. For my part, it could have gone on for a long time, I was quite happy. Dead with exhaustion, but happy. Without desire. Chewing my quid of tobacco. Spitting. Grumbling. Getting back to work. Setting off on yet another whaling trip. Filling up my dixie. All the same, there is a certain satisfaction in killing the whale. The men enjoy the kill. They are proud of themselves. They've caught it! There is rivalry between the crews. The winner is whoever kills the most whales. They were breaking records. Killing.

. . . .

Everybody was covered in blood.

What a weird summer that was!

A windy summer. With terrifying squalls of wind and fog so thick that the horizon was never clear. Port Deception was really at the end of the world. One felt utterly lost there.

One morning in late January a white boat came and dropped anchor amongst us. It was a queer shape, masted as a schooner. It was flying the American flag. Everything on board was made either of wood or of non-magnetic metals. The hull was of oak and Oregon pine, joined with pegs, or tree-nails, of acacia, with a few bronze bolts. The engine itself was made of bronze or copper. Its originality lay in this construction of entirely non-magnetic materials; it did not contain a single particle of steel or iron susceptible to the influence of the magnetic needle. It had sailed into our latitudes for the purpose of studying the phenomena of terrestrial magnetism. Its scientific cruise was destined to take it as far as New Zealand. The ship was the *Carnegie*.

And so it was on board the *Carnegie* that I left Port Deception, after being officially escorted on board by Schmoll, and it was on board the *Carnegie* that I learned that Europe was at war, that the world was at war, that it had been at war for more than six months.

Disembarking at Wellington in September, I immediately enlisted with the Anzacs.

In January 1916 I was on the Somme.

In Cow Wood.

They say the war turned everything upside-down; I believe that, most of all, it turned love upside-down.

.   .   .   .

Cylinder Five

. . . .

Here, Mademoiselle, here is another of Mireille's little exercise books; I found it today in her vanity case, in the secret compartment where Mireille hid her treasures: our marriage certificate, her driving licence, the postcard with the portrait of St Teresa of the Child Jesus with her arms full of roses, her first film contract, a horseshoe, a small nail, a big nail, a four-leafed clover, the photograph of my mother which I gave her, an empty locket, an empty jewel case and a cheque-book in her name which she had never used. There is also a hundred-franc note on which Mireille has written: 'Papa gave this back to me on 8th July 1914.'

Mireille was always afraid of being short of money, which is why I opened a personal account for her with my banker. Mireille never touched that money. She never needed anything. She didn't like spending money. Unlike me, who loved to buy her cars, clothes and all the jewels in the world. But she didn't like jewellery; like my mother, she liked only flowers. I could never buy her enough of them!

Not only did she not use her cheque-book, but Mireille never used her driving licence either. She loved cars, however. I had introduced her to the powerful sports cars. She did not know they existed, nor that one could travel at 140 k.p.h. But she preferred taxis. At the beginning, she would let me drive her, because she loved me and she knew it gave me pleasure to drive fast; but, when she was in a fast car, she had to struggle to control herself. She had to struggle against her own weakness. She suffered from vertigo. From palpitations. And once, a torrent of tears. I had to stop. I thought it was the excitement of speed, but one day she fainted in her seat. I had wanted to buy her an aeroplane; instead, I had to take her to a doctor.

What a disaster! It seemed she was doomed.

They talked to me about a lesion of the heart, but it wasn't that which killed her. She died of another disease, a bizarre disease whose name I have forgotten and which I couldn't describe, a malady they discovered much later, much too late, and in the face of which the doctors were helpless, knowing nothing about it. It was at one and the same time a mental, a mystical and a physical illness, horribly physical. Ah! If I had known, I, who thought it was her purity, I would have taken that illness upon myself, like a beast of burden, if only I had known! I would have cured her. But there, one never knows, and the doctors had already condemned my poor Mireille to death; there was nothing I could do except spoil her as if I were her big brother. No more cars. I coddled her like a poor, fragile little thing. She was in any case my most precious possession. I kept her from all excitement. I adored her. I made her laugh. I always made her laugh.

Naturally Mireille knew nothing about it. She did not know she was ill. She didn't feel ill. Although often uneasy, and even given to fits of acute anxiety, she was gay, always gay. And how sweet she was! We went out now by taxi, gently, gently, and I took her to the cinema. She had a passion for the cinema. That's why I let her act, in spite of the advice of the doctors, who said she must not tire herself.

One day someone introduced me to a character with long hair. He was a film director and, just at that moment, he was looking for a backer. This meeting took place in the hairdresser's salon at the Ritz. I had told Mireille to wait for me in the lobby. We were supposed to go to the Bagatelle for lunch. We had nothing to do, nothing else to do. Like today, it was a first of April.

Mademoiselle, please add at the top of this cylinder that today is 1st April and that I am still in my chalet on the *Plan*.

So, it was 1st April, and I wanted to give Mireille a surprise. I had gone down to the hairdresser's and I had intended to go to Cartier's to choose something for her. They introduced me to this character who was looking for a partner, someone to put up money for a film. He was a nice fellow. I took him to the bar. Since learning that Mireille was ill, I had given up drinking. I tossed back half a dozen cocktails and signed a cheque for six hundred thousand francs. Then I introduced this fellow to Mireille and we went to lunch.

Mireille was mad with joy. She was going to act in a film! All through the meal this gentleman explained the script to her. It was all Greek to me. He talked to her about Edgar Allan Poe; he wanted to film a romanticized version of his life. Mireille was to play a woman who was called now Eleonora, now Ligeia and Ulalume. He was, after all, an artist. He intimidated me. His conversation was brilliant. I smiled to see Mireille so happy. She clapped her hands. She was flushed, pink in the face. She was particularly elegant that day, with a tiny little hat on her head. I ordered champagne to clinch the deal.

Do you go to the cinema, Mademoiselle? Yes, you do, don't you? So you will have seen Mireille, you know her, the star of Mireille Films. I set up a company for her, the Société des Films Mireille. That was a nice surprise for a first of April, don't you agree? Amazing to think that, today, one can set up a company just to please a woman! But none of that was in the least important, as long as she was happy.

The gentleman had asked me for six hundred thousand francs for the first film; by the time it was finished, it cost me six million. But that wasn't of any importance. Mireille was happy. Altogether, I spent thirty or forty million and Mireille was able to make three films before she died. Each one became more and more expensive, sumptuous, magnificent, and the gentleman cut his hair shorter and shorter. But none of that was of any consequence. Mireille was happy. Do you remember her at all, Mademoiselle? She played an inspiring muse, Ophelia-type roles. I didn't understand much about it all, but I must admit that this gentleman had really understood the luminous, delicate, touchingly pure side of Mireille's nature. But why did he always bundle her up in antique dresses when she had so many beautiful, chic modern gowns, and why did he always put a lily in her hand and a crown on her head? In my opinion, Mireille was much too playful for roles of that sort. Another thing I had against that gentlemen was that he never made her laugh; Mireille always had a serious air on the screen, serious, even sad, whereas Mireille's laugh was my life.

But, after all, I mustn't be unjust, I confess I do not like artists as a breed, and that man, with his hair. . . . Well, well . . . I don't like artists because . . . because . . . I knew three in St Petersburg . . . once bitten . . . but that's another story . . . I was about to leave for. . . . Well, in short, Mademoiselle, you can get to work now. This time, I am not sending you Mireille's exercise book, it belongs to her, it's a little red exercise book that I didn't know she had, I'll put it back in its hiding-place. Anyway, I've read the whole thing into the machine for you, all at one stretch, as if I were in a hurry. But this needn't prevent you from sending me your photograph. Thank you, Mademoiselle.

. . . .

Cylinder Five (B)

Mireille's Little Exercise Book (the Red One)

. . . .

WHEN I MET HIM

When I met him, I was a poor, sick little girl, bruised, battered and, as it were, lost. I was a sad little abandoned creature and just went through the motions of living, in my corner. My papa was dead. I was bored. They said it was the war. When Mamma came to visit me, on Thursdays, I always expected something else to happen. I often cried, in my long night-dress. I could not pray. I was always cold in the convent. I would stand still in the long corridors and start to shiver. I was afraid, but often I trembled with emotion, telling myself that someone would come and take me away. It would not be Mamma who took me to the same *pâtisserie* every time to drink hot chocolate, but who? Someone big and strong. I was very frightened; then I would look through the telephone directory to see who my rescuer could be. I would open the heavy book at random and, with my eyes shut, point a finger at a name. I was so excited! I dreamed of all the things that were going to happen to me. . . .

When he came, nothing happened. We looked at each other. It was him! Our hands touched. The whole of Paris was celebrating. He took me and put me in his big army car. We linked arms and off we went. I leaned heavily against him. We set off all together. It was as if we were setting off for ever. We were no longer two people, we were a single being, made to live or die together.

First, we had dinner, together with the others, then we slipped off alone, on foot, along the streets. Nothing existed any more.

He bought me a little gingerbread pig.

Another evening he took me to the theatre and I gave him my programme from the Apollo. I saw nothing of the show, although it was very beautiful. Before that, he had gone back to the front and it was on one of his leaves that he had taken me to the Apollo. When we were together, we were in a world of our own. We were two, two of us living this life that had caused us to suffer so much, and, whenever he rejoined his regiment, we never knew whether we would see each other again.

To be longing for death one day, and then to meet him! And to say to myself: now I can live and suffer still! Yes, I can bear my life now, thanks to him. And what a life, an undreamed of life, we led then! We never said anything to each other, no, we never talked about ourselves. It was years before I knew his real name. He liked to be called Dan Yack, but he had another name, which he finally told me, at the same time making me a present of it. He is always giving me presents. How good he is! But he doesn't like me to tell him about my life. So I have never told him anything about myself. 'Don't say a word, I know it all already, I don't want to know any more about it!' he declares. So I have never told him anything. There have never been confessions between us. There have never been lies. We found ourselves together, that's all, at a moment when neither of us expected anything any more; during the war, time had dragged. . . . My God, to have a life without lies, without disgust, without anything but friendship, a very pure friendship. . . . It doesn't much matter how long it lasts, as long as it exists. And it does! All we did was look at each other, and that's all, ever since the first day. There has never been anything else between us. And there's nothing wrong with this tenderness, o my love!

MY LOVE

My love! With you, I have become a little girl again, with you, I have assuaged my pain. I go to sleep now with no thought in my head but to sleep and, tomorrow, to sing and live again, with you, all our childhood. We play games. How many times have we sung the *Ave* or the *Gloria in excelsis Deo* together! We would start singing when there was no longer a sound in the hotel, and we sang very seriously, in spite of the fact that you imitated all the sounds of the organ, in miming them, to make me laugh. In the end, I had to laugh because you couldn't make me laugh, o my love! And you taught me your own songs. You put an electric torch under the bedclothes and you sang me all your songs. Some of them were very funny; a lot I didn't understand because they were in foreign languages, then you translated them into French for me, imitating all sorts of weird musical instruments and playing the accompaniment on my suspender belt, your silk cravat, two teaspoons which you used as castanets, the back of the chair (beating time with a curtain-rod), the bed-springs, the carpet, armchairs, drawers, your bunch of keys, empty bottles, glasses, my eyebrow-tweezers, my nail-file – you used anything and everything to make music. How happy you were, and how angry I used to get when you made the bathroom taps sing or the trunks and cases bark! I was always afraid you'd wake the whole hotel. They never said anything to us, but in the mornings, when the chambermaid came in and saw the chaos you had created in my room, I used to die of shame.

O my love! After these games, we never had anything more to say to one another. We had no need of words. We were like brother and sister, as if we had been brought up together, with lots of memories in common. I would fall asleep on your lap. You would carry me to bed. I would fall asleep for the second time, all alone in my big bed, and you would sit and watch me sleep. What a strange thing sleep is! I would let myself go utterly, and yet, even if you went back into your room next door to smoke, I knew in my sleep that you were watching over me. I was not afraid; I never had a bad dream; I no longer knew what anguish was. In my mind, I was talking to you. In my sleep, I told you all the things I never managed to say to you during the day. My breath ruffled your hair, in my sleep. In my sleep I confided to you all my secret anxieties and all my worries vanished, in my sleep. I rested. One night I saw you leave in a hurry and, in my sleep, I followed you through the streets. You went to Les Halles to buy flowers. For quite a long time, in my sleep, I felt that you wanted to tell me something, something very important, and that you didn't dare speak for fear of waking me. I didn't wake up, but when you came back with four bunches of carnations, yellow, white, cream, mauve, I was waiting for you on the threshold of my room. I saw you come running. You wanted to say something to me and, in my sleep, I had come to meet you. Seeing you come to me with the flowers . . . did I dream it, or did I really go back to sleep, in my dream? That was my whole answer to whatever you wanted to ask me, o my love! You are my repose, my smile.

TAXIS

Taxis are like little jewel caskets with lovers inside. Taxis are like musical boxes with little birds inside. The lovers do not speak, they murmur with their eyes and say nothing. They live side by side, pressed close, and that is why they are so happy in the taxi.

Lovers do not laugh in a taxi. They do not sing in a taxi. They are serious. They look at one another. They are far away. Mysteriously they squeeze each other's hands as if they were about to exchange something very precious. In love, everything is a surprise. That is why, when the taxi stops, it is always in front of some dazzling shop-window. Then, you buy up the whole shop for me, o my big, crazy man!

CINEMAS

When we weren't lost in a taxi, we lost ourselves in the cinemas. How frightened I was! I didn't know Paris and the taxis sometimes took us much too far; but he, my big man, how did he know all those cinemas he took me to?

In the evenings we often went to the local flea-pits. My love bought tickets for the seats right at the top, amongst the workers. He liked the common people very much. He would light his pipe, talk to the women and kids. I, too, liked these people very much, these people who reminded me of the good folk I used to visit with my papa on his rounds, when I was just a little girl. My big man knew everybody, it was really extraordinary. He chatted to the girl in the box-office, to the usherette, and gave the kids toys he had brought along in his pockets. During the interval he always went down with the men and bought them drinks. It is true, everybody loved him, in all the *quartiers*. It might well have made me jealous.

During the day we went to the big cinemas on the boulevards. He always took a box just for the two of us, a box which he hired for the whole day, and we often stayed there through all the performances, from three in the afternoon till midnight. When there was a film with Louise Fazenda, he hired the box for the whole week and we came every day to clap. My big man had a veritable passion for Fazenda, he unearthed all her films, even those in which she only had a tiny part. He said she was the funniest woman in the world because she didn't play for laughs, she was just naturally gauche. He would have loved to meet her. I was not jealous. He could have gone to meet her.

I loved the cinema. There were lots of serials and we used to go every Friday, and it was marvellous because, on that day, we had episodes from at least a dozen films to see. Amongst others, *La Fin de la Gloire*, with such a pretty woman in it, and a stunning, rascally sort of Foreign Legionnaire, who appealed to my love because of his tattoos. And, together, we very much admired Irene Castle, who played the role of a millionairess in a very complicated film. My big man said he had never seen a woman who wore clothes with such style and flair as she did. Irene never made another film, but I have not forgotten her hazel eyes, nor the way she walked. She crossed a drawing-room, or Broadway, like a swan rippling the surface of a pond, always majestic, solitary, simple. My love said she glided like a sailing-ship. Once, on the rue des

Blancs-Manteaux, we saw a film without title, without the director's or the actors' names, a film which must have been taken from the story of Fausta, but it was about a Fausta who lived in a caravan in some frontier zone, in a northern landscape in the rain. God, how beautiful that film was, and that woman made me cry! My big man loved it too, but she made him laugh because, in one pathetic scene, she chewed on an unlit cigar and, in another, she beat her sister black and blue, using a big whip which she wielded like a carter, a feat that won her my big man's admiration. Her sister was an ugly little black shrew who was always wishing her ill and who was jealous, so jealous; the Fausta was tall, a little weary, a little overripe, and, in her rather faded face, she had an eye with a slight cast in it, like Réjane, but she was much better than Réjane, whose film *Miarka, La Fille à l'Ours*, had just been shown in a cinema on the boulevards. She was much better because she was anonymous. My love claimed she was Danish, because she looked like a Danish sailor he had once employed. It is true there was something mannish about this woman. She drank a lot and looked people straight in the eye, like a man. We used to go and see Charlie Chaplin's films in a cinema near the Gare de Lyon. It had once been a restaurant, a big, wood-panelled room that looked like the inside of a piano and resounded when the audience laughed their heads off at Charlie. This audience, which laughed so loud, with a roar like a steam train entering a station, was made up for the most part of railway workers enjoying their day off, and bareheaded girls. There, too, my big man drank with everybody. One drink, or a snack, entitled you to watch one number in the programme, and you had to buy several if you wanted to see it right through to the end. They always showed documentaries and newsreels which you never saw in any other cinema in Paris. Charlie Chaplin's films were an extra, so you had to take another double *consommation* to watch them at the end of the round. We always ate cherries in brandy, two portions each. Ah, if Charlie had known! He would have come and drunk a toast with us, and with those delirious railwaymen, to honour the triumph of Monsieur Nouvel-An, 'Mister New Year', his double.

Monsieur Nouvel-An was the owner of the cinema-bistro. On the programme, he announced himself as:

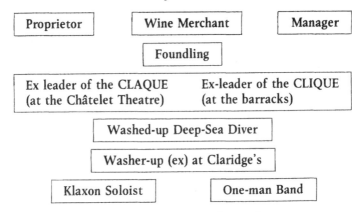

Monsieur BENJAMIN NOUVEL-AN

| Proprietor | Wine Merchant | Manager |

| Foundling |

| Ex leader of the CLAQUE (at the Châtelet Theatre) | Ex-leader of the CLIQUE (at the barracks) |

| Washed-up Deep-Sea Diver |

| Washer-up (ex) at Claridge's |

| Klaxon Soloist | One-man Band |

Inimitable Imitator of Sounds

The SPITTING IMAGE of CHARLIE CHAPLIN

appearing

! ! ! IN THE FLESH ! ! !

My love, who was very fond of this man, invited him to lunch one day. In public, he was a sad, taciturn man with staring eyes, eyes like a bird's, a man who drank without saying a word; but at home, he was liberated: juggling with fifty different musical instruments, which he played all at once, he set up a delirious racket, a joyful, raucous music. As a mimic of sounds, he was a veritable virtuoso, which is why his programmes included documentaries and newsreels he chose personally so as to give free rein to his talent and his imagination. He made the sound of the wind, the rain, the full moon, the night, the storm, the hurricane; the noises of machines, the telescopic effect of a train approaching and then fading into the distance, the purr of an aeroplane engine, the brouhaha of the crowd in the street, or at the exit from the Métro, a house burning down, every kind of animal, male and female, all the birds, *ad lib*, the sea, the ocean; and he could imitate, like nobody else, the ringing of the telephone, the crackle on the line, the interrupted conversations, or a gun battle. For

Charlie's films, he improvised zany, irresistible sketches, With his voice alone, he imitated all the contortions, all the acrobatics of Charlie and his cast, as well as the pathetic moments, when there was a pause in the action to allow for a big close-up of Charlie's face, disconcerted, frozen, bewildered, thunderstruck, with that oh-so-sad smile, or a double take, or his expression when he is disarmed and distressed, having come face to face with the nastiness of fate, or again, when he falls down, when life has suddenly clipped his wings. Monsieur Nouvel-An found words that were so funny they made you cry. The little bowler, the baggy pants, the walking-stick, the running away, the falling down, the sliding, the unstable balance, the thirst, the hunger, the love – each of Charlie's individual traits had its own voice, its special intonation, its accent and its timbre. Monsieur Nouvel-An knew how to capture the grimaces, the blows, the slaps, the alarming about-turns, the angelic astonishment; he even succeeded in rendering Charlie's gait, and the turned-out feet, with his voice. His masterpiece was the sketch he embroidered for 'Charlie the Night-Owl', where, without words, without a single sentence or a single comment, with nothing but the sounds – the grinding of the key in the lock, the tick-tock of the clock, the slipping of rugs from under his feet, the creaking of furniture, the breaking of crockery, the fall of an object, the treacherous turn of the stairs, the hiccups, the bumping into things, the sighs, the echo of furtive steps and a sudden gallop – he managed to make you share in the mortal breakdown, the despair, the helplessness, the terror of the drunkard. As my love said, Monsieur Nouvel-An was the precursor, the virtual inventor of talking pictures and of the sound-track. He died last year in a violent attack of delirium, and my big man was the only person who followed his coffin. It was very sad. In the big cinemas on the boulevards we would go to see Rio Jim, Charles Ray, Louise Glaum, Fatty Arbuckle, Pauline Frederick, Bessie Love, Lillian Gish in *The Broken Lily*, and the first Mack Sennett comedies. Apart from his passion, the unforgettable Louise Fazenda, these were the only American stars my big man admired. 'All the others', he said, 'are liars and cheats. What they do is just gimmickry.'

Another little cinema, which I nearly forgot, was installed in a church in Batignolles. They showed English films, which were absurd, but my big man enjoyed going there, not to see the film but to sleep. In fact, it was the only place where I ever saw him sleep. On Sundays the place was occupied by some Methodist sect or other, but during the week it was rented out to the cinema, so we would take a pew, my love would wrap his arms round me and soon fall asleep to the lullaby of the tangos, the foxtrots, the shimmies and all the fashionable dances which a blind man played on the harmonium. My big man woke up only during the stage show, to watch the antics of the trained dogs or the pathetic little girl singers. One evening a sailor came and boxed with a kangaroo, and my dear man was absolutely determined to buy this kangaroo. All night long we walked it up and down, then, before going back home to the Ritz, we set it free in the place Vendôme.

The last film we saw together - a little while before I started acting in films myself and we no longer had time to go to other people's films - was *Victory Parade*. I remember that, when we left the cinema, we started singing in the taxi. At the tops of our voices. We were as happy as a couple of kids, happy to be together, happy to have survived all that, happy to be alive. We kissed each other.

MY BIG MAN

You are my repose, my smile.
Since knowing you, I no longer suffer.
I am not ill any more.

I don't know how you've done it, but, just as you promised, you have taken my illness upon yourself. You've cured it! I no longer feel my heart, my heart that used to give me so much pain. I am no longer anxious, I can breathe.

Now, there is just one thing I fear: you, you who drink too much. I dare not say anything to you about it, but I know that, one day, you will stop drinking, just as you have already sold all your sports cars to please me.

When I look at you, I wonder . . . no, I cannot ask, any more than I can pray . . . I love you!

. . . .

Cylinder Five (C)

Mireille's Little Exercise Book (the Red One, continued)

.   .   .   .

MY FILMS

He had set up a company in my name, the Société des Films Mireille, so that I could make films, and he had given me a tortoise. He called this tortoise Chewing Gum, and I took her everywhere with me. She was my mascot. In the sleeping-car, when we left for Seville or Vienna, where we were to shoot some scenes, I put her on the luggage-rack, with her salad and the cigarettes for my love. In spite of this, I started to be afraid of life once more. I didn't really like going abroad, I felt good only when we were back home in Paris, at the Ritz, but I had to go on location, and besides, I enjoyed the shooting so much. I was on my way to becoming a film star - oh, what joy!

Everyone was very kind to me: M. Lefauché, my director, Marc Sévère, my leading man; the adorable Madeleine Yveline, from the Comédie des Champs-Elysées, who was my co-star.

In Seville we shot one episode for *The Life of Edgar Allan Poe* in the gardens of the Alcázar, and in Vienna one for *The Tales of Hoffmann* in the ex-Imperial Palace. I loved this film about Edgar Allan Poe, which was my screen début and brought me into the most beautiful gardens in Europe: the Alcázar, the larger-than-life artificial garden belonging to Lord Stuff, in London, the Roman gardens of Otto Kahn, the banker, at Cap Martin, the walled gardens of the Hôtel de Ville in Coutances, the hanging gardens of Isola Bella, and the Japanese garden, where everything is in miniature, belonging to Mme Danita Sterne. In this film all I had to do was walk through all these gardens. It was difficult and not in the least monotonous. In my robes, my long, trailing or transparent robes, I personified the thoughts of Edgar Allan Poe, and all these gardens represented his various states of mind. My big man said to me: 'If you have to hurry, walk naturally, like the tortoise. Take a good look at her, you will see she is actually hurrying. If you are to walk slowly, your graceful movements must make the audience think of a fan. Don't forget Irene Castle and her gliding like a sailing-ship, nor Louise Fazenda, the scatterbrain, bouncing about like a tennis ball.'

In this film I also had to walk on the bottom of the sea. They had taken me to see the aquarium in Monaco and the one in Naples to study the undulations of the fish and the algae; I was to descend to the bottom of the sea in a secret cove in Capri, a cove with pure water and the lovely vegetation of algae and sponges, and M. Lefauché had had some beautiful big luminous corals made, which had already been placed between the tufts of subaquatic plants around which I had to dance, but I was suddenly seized with unreasoning terror and a terrible hammering of the heart, and I refused absolutely to shoot this scene. The whole unit had to pull up stakes once again, the electricians, the camera crew, the actors, the specialists who had been called in to dress the set on the bottom of the sea, everyone went back to Paris, to work in the studio, which was rapidly transformed into an underwater garden, with a special arrangement of pools with false bottoms, equipped with screens of distorting glass. which enabled them to set up the lighting and shoot from the sides and from below, and with a machine to create waves. A special device allowed an instant change-over to slow motion or speeding up. Apparently all this cost a fortune. Everyone was furious with me, and M. Lefauché most of all. He became very stern with me, even unfair, claiming that I had sabotaged his ideas and that I was incapable of understanding and carrying out his most inspired strokes of genius. I was confused, but I am afraid of water, I have always been afraid of water; it is an innate fear. I truly believe I would have died of a heart attack if I had had to go down into that cove. I have forgotten to say that, in Capri, I would have had to shoot inside a glass diving-bell, lit and driven by electricity, and that, in the studio, Anna Kellermann doubled for me in all the underwater scenes. I felt a little ashamed when I saw her diving, swimming, frolicking in the water as if it were her natural element and playing my role, but it seems this is quite a common practice in the cinema; they showed her only from the back or in soft focus, because, while our figures are more or less the same, Anna's face is round, mine is a beautiful oval, and there is a great difference in our ages. My big man (who, however, was not very keen on this stunt with Kellermann, although he never said a cross word to me) was the only one who believed that everything worked equally well this way. Just the same, I was annoyed with myself for having been afraid, so much so that all the last part of that film gave me a great deal of trouble.

In *The Tales of Hoffmann* I had a much pleasanter time. Nobody asked me to perform such prodigious feats. I was the Imagination, or Fantasy, personified as a sprite, an imp, a mischievous familiar, a mocking little goblin who is always tormenting Hoffmann. I was supposed to haunt his musical instruments, his scores, books and papers, and to upset his sedentary and home-loving habits, making him travel far away on a beam of sunlight, dragging him with me through the wreathing smoke from his pipe, smiling at him, making him fall over, and drowning him at the bottom of his glass as if I had carried him up to the sky and dropped him into it. It was charming and sometimes very funny. I appeared in the form of a sylph, as the Queen of Sheba, a haughty princess, Cinderella, a fairy, a sorceress, a good little servant-girl, maddening and elusive, staining his window-panes so that he would see the world in blue, lending him glasses with double lenses so that he could read people's thoughts, passing him his tobacco-jar full of such strong snuff that each sneeze carried him to the other side of the world, the dark side, handing him his pen which then transformed itself into a bow and putting a violin into his hands which, if he was unlucky enough to start playing it, turned into a full moon, dripping with blood, while the bow pierced his heart and he was metamorphosed into a bird, a nightingale singing his heart out in front of a rose, and, once again, it was I who appeared as the rose.

This beautiful romantic film would have given me great pleasure if, in the long run, it had not worried me. At that time Vienna was unhealthy and full of phantasmagoria. The people were suffering from hunger, there was wildly spiralling inflation and everything imaginable in the way of disorder, shady dealings, tragic love affairs, bloody passions, dramas, loneliness, sombre shadows and a kind of heaviness, and everything, all the stories one heard in that newly deserted Imperial Palace, already hired out to a film company, everything, even down to the open bottle of scent I found one day in an empty cupboard in the bedroom of the hapless Zita, afflicted me and made me anxious, nervous and sad. In the evenings my big man, for all his affection and tenderness, had great difficulty in getting me to sleep. No matter how lovingly he tucked me in, or took me in his arms - our lovely nocturnal musical sessions had ended long ago - I was feverish. I tossed and turned in my bed. In an uneasy half-sleep I saw Hoffmann walking over my eyelids. It was no longer Marc Sévère playing the role, but a cunning gypsy, handsome and swarthy, with a gleaming skin. He played the violin to me, passionately, and his eyes illuminated my room fitfully, like the 'Jupiter' arc lamps in the studio when the carbons ignite. He hypnotized me. At last I would go to sleep, but, in my sleep, I stretched out my hand to him and this great devil of a Bohemian, growing blacker and blacker, more and more brilliant, more and more ungainly, more and more passionate, fiery and insistent, all teeth and eyes, seized hold of it to read the lines on my palm. We were pressed close together, our two heads bent over my hand as we traced the pulsating network of lines. I asked him . . . I asked him . . . 'Will I die soon, Carol?' He was called Carol in my dreams, Carol and another name, much tenderer and sweeter, which is always on my lips during sleep, but which I can never remember when I wake, even though I make prodigious efforts of memory, for, while everything else comes back to me from this dream - my anxiety, my emotion, my fever and even the very vague awareness of the presence of my love, who is smoking in the next room, this little nickname, this tender, melting little name eludes me. 'Carol, will I die soon. . . ?'

I see the laughing gypsy nod his head, raise his eyebrows, pull a face, and I distinctly hear him click his tongue, with an unpleasant sound, while his hard black thumbnail scratches a cross on my lifeline, tickling me and making me shiver. When I wake up, I am always ill and feel convinced I am going to die soon. I have never told my big man anything about this dream, but it was from that time, a little before filming ended, that I began to imagine I was really ill.

After this film M. Lefauché was once more very kind, he had regained his confidence in me; he even claimed that I was extraordinarily sensitive and that, if they let him do it, he would draw some superhuman performances out of me. I was, he said, the actress he had always dreamed of.

M. Lefauché was certainly exaggerating, he did so because he wanted to flatter me, and he wanted to flatter me because, at that moment, he was acting with me. It was my third film. I played an artificial woman and M. Lefauché played the inventor, so we did all our scenes together. He was bringing to the screen Villiers de l'Isle-Adam's masterpiece, *L'Eve Future*. My big man was very displeased to see me in this role of an artificial woman constructed by an inventor who animates her, little by little, to the point where he can actually breathe life into her. However, my performance was phenomenal, that was the unanimous opinion, not only of M. Lefauché, who was in raptures, and of the film unit, but also of the audiences in every capital in the world, who turned this film into a triumph. Only my fellow-artistes and the film crew knew what it had cost me. They had watched me suffer, they had seen me repeat, a hundred times over, not a dramatic scene but the mere sketch of a simple gesture or a borrowed movement and, even less than that, just the ghost of a simple pulsation: for example, the first flutter of movement in the eyelids and the first dilatation of the pupils (and I was clever enough to squeeze a tear out first, before letting just one glance escape). For months and months I suffered like a martyr, I had to hold my breath, stop my circulation, put a brake on all my senses so as to appear pallid, inanimate, devoid of feeling, for the whole of the time that the artificial woman was being brought to perfection. I should never have been able to achieve this total shedding of my own personality, this neutralization of my whole being, this latent lifelessness, this prefiguration of a kind of mystical death, which I was able to portray on the screen, if it had not been for my heart disease and that obscure, intimate derangement which was gaining a stronger and stronger hold on me.

It is only fair to include M. Lefauché in this triumph. From the beginning to the end of the film his technique and his photography were impeccable. Without him I should perhaps never have been able to touch the hearts of the public in the scenes where the future Eve remained in a state of automatism, unconscious, passive, waiting, lost, before she was connected to human consciousness, nor in the later scenes of insatiable appetite, temptations, stubbornness, sensuality, sadness, when the artificial Eve comes to life and begins to live, really to live, with the heart of a woman; but, on the other hand, he exhausted me, because M. Lefauché went too far. For instance, he knew how to make me cry, how to make me weep real tears for the close-ups. Once he discovered this faculty, he abused it. My tears were no longer enough for him, I must weep, sob, hiccup with nerves. He reduced my whole innermost being to a state of prostration and profound desolation. These sessions wore me out. Then he would push me to the limit, and, when I couldn't bear it any more, when I was about to faint, he would force me to go on for a moment longer, driving me to the point of collapse, so that he could turn his monstrous lens on me, use the cruellest lighting in the studio to expose my weakness and film me in the last stages of exhaustion. If I fell on my knees, he made me crawl, and I would hear him yell into the megaphone: 'That's very good, darling, it's great like that!' He was sincere, and shouted so loudly that I would have been justified in feeling very proud of myself, but for the fact that my weariness was not simulated, it was real, and insinuating itself ever more deeply into me.

I realize that the interpretation of every role involves a good deal of exaggeration, especially in the expression of those feelings to which the vulgar crowd is sensitive. Because of the immense audiences the cinema attracts, directors feel obliged to do everything on a grand scale to capture the public's attention. Today, film-making is a rivalry of colossal expenditure, box-office receipts, publicity, an orgy of electricity, sumptuous costumes, casts of thousands, sensational stars and spectacular scenes. This arbitrary and supposedly commercial concept of the cinema has created an occupational disease amongst directors which expresses itself, in the overall product as much as in the minute details of their work, through a whole series of cock-eyed monstrosities, sublimities, incongruities, phoney situations, implausibilities and prodigious feats so stupendous and absurd that human reason seems to have been banished for ever. A film is a hotchpotch in which the best, by chance, rubs shoulders with the worst. These criticisms come from my big man, who was in the habit of adding that M. Lefauché, for all his talent, was not without a touch of that megalomania which seems to be the attribute, the mental vice, of people in the film business. I have already said that my big man did not like M. Lefauché very much. He reproached him with a certain self-importance and grandiloquence, with ponderousness and slowness, and a complete lack of any sense of reality. He said to me: 'All that symbolism just covers up his paucity of ideas. Everything he makes you do is false.'

My big man loved to make me laugh and to see me carefree and gay. He had a horror of these complicated roles. He loved my simplicity, my innate sobriety. 'It's all idiotic,' he said, still talking about these extraordinary roles M. Lefauché chose to cast me in, 'it's all idiotic and unhealthy. You should come back into real life.' I do not know who was right, because if carefree gaiety, childishness and a certain naïveté share my heart, I believe that, at bottom, my true nature is really sadness. I have always been sad, mortally sad when I was a little girl, with those attacks of anxiety which would suddenly grip my heart, and when I sensed that I was going to faint, I would quickly, quickly, burst out laughing. That is why I can laugh at will, but my laughter always hurts me, though this is something I have always kept hidden from my big man.

He had been so good to me! He had inspired me with such confidence. He had known how to take me in his arms. He had known how to calm me. He had known how to take my illness upon himself. I no longer felt my heart. I was no longer afraid of anything. Before acting in the cinema I had become very strong. He made me eat and drink, and he knew how to get me to sleep. I breathed easy. I was calm. And it was all thanks to my dear man.

Besides, I owe him everything. Everything I know, I have learned from him. He taught me to dress. He taught me to walk. He taught me how to make up. I must admit that, without him, I should never have been able to do what I did in *L'Eve Future*. In the evenings, after working at the studio, he went over all the advice, all the direction, all the suggestions M. Lefauché had given me, on the pretext that they were nothing but professional gimmicks, and he started miming the scenes I had already shot, or still had to shoot. Everything he suggested to me was radiant, easy and natural, it was the truth itself, always the full reality. He was extraordinary. He would carry to perfection a gesture I had managed only to sketch in. I would explain to him the situation as M. Lefauché had explained it to me, and my dear man would immediately find not only the expression, the arrangement of the features, the look in the eyes, the unfolding of the smile that would best render this or that emotion, but the movements of the body, the slowed down reaction of the muscles, or that quickening of the nerves which vitalizes a person's behaviour to the point of giving him a striking, even a dancing presence. 'Balance is in movement,' he said, 'if you're not moving, you're posing. That's all there is to it. That's the whole secret of the cinema.'

When I asked him where he had learned all this, he replied that he had never needed to study acting, but that he had observed all these feelings and expressions amongst men in everyday life. 'You have only to look around you in the street,' he said, 'to see that every passer-by is a brother. Follow this man, ape him, imitate his walk, adopt his mannerisms, dress like he does and you will see that there is no mystery, you will be surprised to find that you end up thinking like he does. As for women, they are nothing but pretence. All you have to do, to find out what they are really like, is the exact opposite of whatever they're doing. I know of only two women who are disinterested, Fazenda and you. You should be making a different kind of film.'

He started re-enacting all the roles we had admired together at the cinema. He imitated various actors, played their parts, and explained to me why Charles Ray, after shooting himself in the mouth when the Vamp ordered him out of her house, slid under the table in just such a way and no other. 'It was', he said, 'so as not to die instantly, to have enough strength left to crawl on all fours for a moment, like an animal, to drag himself up to the feet of this woman who has been his destiny, to raise his eyes, already filled with death, once more to her face, and force one last smile out of his torn mouth before vomiting up all his blood: *he no longer wants to vomit blood, he wants to render up his soul.*'

'It's only a question of the angle,' he added after a moment's reflection.

'Now, you must be equal to the demands of this machine,' my dear man said to me when we talked about the film camera. And he taught me, all over again, how to walk, geometrically, for the crystalline eye of the lens and not for the sensibilities of the human eye.

'We're going to make you do something very simple!' he cried jubilantly.

After the great success of *L'Eve Future* M. Lefauché came to see him and discuss my next film. He wanted to do *A Midsummer Night's Dream*, but my big man got very angry.

'Haven't you had enough of shooting these idiotic things?' he shouted. 'Are you trying to kill her? Can't you see that these roles of yours exhaust the poor child?'

M. Lefauché had not expected this outburst, and, seeing the amazement on his face, my love smiled at him and said: 'We want something very simple, my friend. Listen, I've got an idea. What do you think of "Simple Simon"?'

SIMPLE SIMON

Now that I am in bed, now that I am ill, I know quite well I shall never finish this film, *Simple Simon*. As soon as we started shooting the first scenes, I knew that I shouldn't be able to carry on. It was so much *me*, myself, that I felt as if I was acting stark naked, morally naked.

No, no, no, I beg you, go away, I can't, I won't do it!

You don't love me, you're a monster, your love is nothing but pity.

The screen does not lie, I saw myself.

That's enough! I understand now what you wanted.

O my love, how you frightened me!

My God, how could he have known that I was dying to play the part of a boy? How did he manage to see so deeply into me? I had never spoken to him about it and I thought this longing of mine was well hidden, deep in my innermost self.

Since my very earliest childhood I have always wanted to be a boy. I never wanted to play with dolls, I never had a doll or, if somebody happened to give me one, I quickly chopped off her hair and dressed her as a man, then I would go and hide her, shamefacedly, in one of the cupboards in the granary. I was so afraid Papa would discover my secret. And now my love has found me out! I don't want to see him any more, I should die of shame.

My papa was tall and strong, with lovely fair hair and blue eyes. I did everything I could to be like him. He didn't treat me like a little girl, I was his chum, which is why I loved him so much. He called me his 'little cabin-boy' and made me feel very proud. How strong and pure was my love for my father! Mamma never bothered about me. She didn't understand me, she didn't know who I was. I saw her after Papa's death, when she took me - how heart-breaking! - to a convent school. I have never loved my mother. I don't want to know what she did. If I had been a boy, I shouldn't even have gone out with her on Thursdays, when she came to fetch me. At night, in the convent, I used to dress up as a man. I made a man's costume out of anything and everything that came to hand and I dragged my hair back tight, tight, with a parting at the side. As there were no mirrors in my little room, I couldn't admire myself, but still I was delighted to be able just to sit there in the dark, dressed as a man, and amuse myself inventing my friends, my comrades and a fiancé. I reviewed all the names I had chosen from the telephone directory, and my fiancé was always a kind of big brother who looked like Papa. Before I'd even seen him, I loved him very much. And when he came to fetch me, with all the others, I immediately chose Dan Yack. He was tall, strong, with very fair hair and beautiful blue eyes. It was him, my big man, my friend, my saviour.

O my love!

You, too, have always treated me like a chum; but I don't want to see you any more, because I am ashamed and you frighten me.

O my love, I am afraid of you!

You are good. Nothing discourages you, neither my nerves, nor my obsessions, nor my unreasonable fears, nor my clumsiness. You are kind to me because you are good. You keep my mind off my worries because you are good. You amuse me because you are good. You spoil me. But none of that is done out of love, or you would never have made me play Simple Simon, you who know me so well that now I am afraid of you. Oh, how miserable am I! Poor Mireille!

How awkward I felt, how ashamed, trapped up there on the screen! I felt sorry for myself, and the more Simple Simon's carelessness, clumsiness and imbecility were shown up, the more jubilant my big man became, and the whole film unit, who also came to watch the rushes, clapped. I was the only one to be touched by this poor, wretched ninny, and to realize that he was irremediably lost. Life wounded him, everything came to grief, nothing made any sense to him. Everything he tried to do rebounded on him, crushed him, suffocated him, every one of his thoughts became an obsession against which he knocked his head in vain, and yet he was moved by grand intentions! Everybody laughed at his misfortunes, he was the only person who did not find them at all amusing. That is why, on a rainy day, he jumps into the water to avoid getting wet, and why he throws himself with total abandon into heroic, ridiculous, imaginary adventures which are always abortive, and the last of which kills him. I wept bitterly. And yet it was not the first time I had seen myself on the screen. This time, however, I was not playing a part any more, I saw myself revealed to myself, it was I myself whom I saw evolving – me, me, just as I am and just as I confess myself to be: loony, bewildered, clumsy, fearful, stubborn, with a wild desire for grandeur and purity, and so helpless, incompetent, powerless, stupid. Poor Simple Simon! A sort of *fille manquée*, a boy who was meant to be a girl. I shall die of shame.

O my big man, forgive me! I am nothing but a *fille manquée*! I did not mean to do wrong when I always refused to give myself to you; on the contrary, I was very proud of myself and imagined I was being very big and strong.

What an imbecile!

Poor Mireille!

I understand everything. Everything amuses you. You laugh. I cry. Your strength and your grandness of spirit are only a game. I no longer want to give you cause to pity me, and, out of the generosity of your soul, indulge my slightest caprices, the caprices of a bewildered little girl. What is the good of loving me, if you bring yourself down to the level of my worst failings? I am nothing but a *fille manquée*.

Enough!

I don't want to, I don't want to, I don't want to.

. . . .

Cylinder Six

. . . .

The chalet on the Plan, 21st April 1925

Night time. It's raining. It has been raining for a week. For a week, I have done nothing. I stand in front of my window and look out. Outside, it's raining. The wind blows the smoke back into the room in gusts. So I open my door, take a dozen steps outside, in the rain, and come in again, shut the door and plant myself once more in front of the window. I look out. Outside, it's raining.

I lie down two or three times during the day. I am very weary. I fall asleep at once. In my sleep I hear the birds. I wake up immediately. I go back and plant myself in front of my window. I look out. Outside, it's raining.

Then, it's night. Black night. I do not light my lamp. I stand there in the dark and look out. It's still raining. I listen. I listen to the wind.

The night is black, black like those nights at the front, when I would stand in the mud and look out through my loophole. The night was black, the night was long, I listened to the wind, the rain trickled down my neck, and, when I dozed off, I still heard the birds. I would wake with a start. I was stuck there, planted in the mud. I looked out through the loophole. There was nothing to be seen. It was black. I listened to the wind. The rain lashed down.

O my mother, you whom I would have loved so much! I think of you. I never knew you. I pull my chair forward and sit astride it, my arms resting on the back and my chin resting on my hands. I glue my forehead to the window and look out. On the velvety backcloth of the night your features appear one by one and stand out as if from an old photograph. First, your mouth, large, shapely and slightly asymmetrical or askew. Above, there is a big nose and, below, a long chin with a dimple. The weight of your hair, black, heavy, thick, like the limbo you have come from, pulls your head back and this makes you stretch your neck, which is of a nebulous whiteness, a whiteness in which I find a resemblance to the white skin of my own neck. Your forehead is extraordinarily pure, transparently innocent, but it is your eyes that disturb me, your eyes, your cheekbones and your temples. You have the same slanting eyes as I have; the left eye, slightly smaller, has a searching look and the right, wide open, seems not to see but to listen, which gives to our physiognomy an overall aspect, an air not of haughtiness but of absence, and to our look something distant and aloof. But while I have almost no cheekbones and you can see large, prominent veins, knotted and twisted, beating on my temples, thus giving a ravaged air to that part of my face (not to mention the handful of freckles my outdoor life has thrown in my face, especially around the eyes, plus a few scars), your temples are smooth, flawless, sloping and lofty, and your cheekbones are prominent. All the upper part of your face appears emaciated, cold and burning, radiant and livid, as if you were wearing some strange kind of half-mask, a black velvet mask made, internally, of glowing embers, of flames, of passion, and, externally, of a hard although feverish serenity (hard because probably hard won, and feverish because feverishly defended), which gives a severe look to your smile, which emerges just where your half-mask ends, and sharpens all your visible features; but there is a true humility in your smile, and this attenuates what would otherwise have been a too trenchant severity. Such destitution, such reserve, such a total knowledge of the self, of all your resources, such a complete acceptance, modified by a touch of malice in the eye and an ironic comma at the corners of the lips, such shy resolution, such complete abandon to the illness that is consuming you, such coldness, such determined muteness, such utter indifference to the insults life has to offer . . . up until now, I have never been able to read all that except on the parchment-like faces of the half-starved lobster-fishermen who sail the coasts of Morocco, and who are, at one and the same time, saints, damned souls, philosophers and scoundrels. What is the secret of this mocking resignation? Is it the punishment of a surfeited soul who knows the taste of all things, who has enjoyed everything and despised everything, or is it the irritability of an insatiable organism in decline? Is it torture or beatitude? Amongst the lobster fishermen this ambiguity is an indication of their profound physiological poverty, but you, o my mother, were you a mystic? I know nothing about you, except for a few inconsequential anecdotes from the time when you were a little girl, and this idiosyncrasy of temperament that led you to live under the sunny skies of Italy, but in the shade, cloistered in your hotel suite.

It was our old Christie who told me about it. It seems you could no longer bear the light of day. The sun got on your nerves. You had the shutters closed. You lived in the hotel in Florence, stretched out on a large sofa of Russia leather, surrounded by candlesticks overburdened with candles, and your beloved flowers. Your life was a secret. Nobody ever knew why you lived like that. You died of a disease of the spinal cord. When they made an inventory of your belongings, they found a card index with the complete nomenclature of all the plants you loved. No one had ever guessed that you had devoted yourself to botanical studies, and that you knew Linnaeus's classifications by heart. Was it a need to forget, simple curiosity, or an invalid's whim that made you attach a Latin name to the names of all your cherished flowers, or was it perhaps a final deception, a pose to throw people off the scent, to make them believe you were devoted to study and not suspect that you were possibly seeking suicide amongst all those poisonous exhalations, those embalming essences, those clinging perfumes that gave you a migraine and sent you into trances and transports?

How funereal your hotel room is, lit by candles, with bouquets wilting in every corner, all those petals falling silently on to the carpets, an avalanche of flowers disintegrating in the darkness of your suite! Outside, there is sunshine on the Arno and the sound of street cries. You will die alone and without a word, without a single complaint during your slow dying. Were you resigned or mad? O my dear mother, what does that interminable list of Latin names signify?

The birds wake me with a start. Was I asleep, then? I look out of the window. Outside, it's raining. Here, as at the front, the dawn is slow in coming. Avalanches thunder down. It's raining. Shadows like clouds of soot rise heavily. It is the dawn unravelling. Tattered clouds eddy in the rags of wet light. And yet it is spring, for a bird has just alighted on a stone. It was a crow with a red beak; he let out his raucous cry and flew away. And now here are three snow buntings in front of my door. They are chirping. I keep quite still. They chirp, then fly away. It's raining. The wind is blowing. That's all. I smile. It is spring.

At the front, too, little birds would come and perch on the barbed wire and, in spite of the rain, in spite of the north wind, they sang. They announced the spring to us. Even then, when the wild flowers no longer grew, because the earth between the lines was so churned up, the birds sang. I remember that when we stormed Vimy Ridge a lark was warbling its heart out. I stopped in my tracks. While my comrades were already tumbling into the German trenches, full of explosions, cries and carnage, I stopped in this rush towards death, I stopped to listen to this lark singing. It was hovering in the air, a stone's throw away. The trajectory of the bullets, bits of shrapnel, shells, the fire from the machine-gun barrage was weaving an invisible cage all around it. The bird flapped its wings and sang. I smiled, dazzled. It was a trilling love-song. Spring.

. . . .

If there exists anywhere in this world a Land of Tenderness, it seems at first sight to be New Zealand. On these favoured isles great flocks of pedigree sheep and cattle graze the tender grass in the small valleys. From one end of the year to the other, nothing comes to disturb them. You can travel by car for days, or on horseback for weeks, without ever meeting a living soul; you can cross peaks, descend again into new valleys, without ever leaving the pasture-lands. Apart from a petrified cataract, a wild corner that looks like a miniature Switzerland (and is reserved for newly-weds who come to spend their honeymoon there, or old couples who come to celebrate their golden wedding anniversary), and what little remains of the primitive flora of the country – a few groves of rare and curious tropical plants, notably the giant cruciferous ferns, which are as flourishing here as in Ceylon – nothing picturesque ever strikes the eye. The whole of the interior of the country is divided into rectangles by high fences, with five strands of barbed wire, which separate the pastures; valley dovetails into valley, hill follows hill, nothing comes to interrupt the uniformity, the monotony of the gleaming grass spread everywhere, this dark-green grass which reflects the sky like water, dominates the landscape and gives it an aspect of calm, repose, peace and a warm silence.

With a little bit of luck, you might chance to stumble upon a cluster of tall eucalyptus trees full of the cooing of doves, and, sheltering beneath their shade, a farm, if you can call this brand-new bungalow a farm, inhabited as it is by a colonist rather than a peasant, and a middle-class housewife rather than a farmer's wife; they dress for dinner every evening, he in a dinner jacket, she in an evening gown, to play the pianola together or huddle over the radio.

This couple is always very young looking, although it's often an old-established household, where the boys are passionately devoted to sport and the young girls cling superstitiously to the social conventions and to the protocol of French etiquette in the colleges and clubs on the coast. Tens of thousands of similar couples are scattered about the solitude of the country, leading exactly the same respectable and well-to-do life from one year to another, and no external event ever comes to disturb the monotonous and sublime course of their sentimentality. Time has passed. They have grown old without realizing it. But they have preserved all the illusions of the heart and the vigour of the senses. They live à deux. For themselves. Egotistical and complacent.

Thus, the mentality of each New Zealander is insular several times over, because each couple is isolated in their own personal feeling of contentment, each farm is a Robinson Crusoe's island amidst the solitude of the pastures, and the twin islands, which appear like a double oasis on the waters, are not welcoming, but close ranks and defend themselves fiercely against any immigration.

New Zealand has broken her moorings and remains in contact with the rest of the world only through a moral link that attaches her to Great Britain, of which country every New Zealander is immeasurably proud to be a distant descendant, thus adding a feeling of pride to his insularity and confirming him in his rejection of all human fraternization.

This situation, which in effect resembles a Utopia, has created a race that believes itself to be pure and of superior essence, because it is strictly selected and there is no cross-breeding, no mixing of the blood. But was not this exclusivity, which seems to give them a right to these feelings of superiority and purity, and to support the convictions of this elect little clan of the white race, equally an attribute, and indeed the salient feature, of the ancient aboriginal race of the Australian islanders, of those savage tribes whom the New Zealanders, in their crazy pride, exterminated by fire and sword in less than twenty-five years? This success, this maintaining of a precarious civilization at the furthest ends of the earth, this specialized and material activity, this total absence of moral grandeur, this lack of ambition, this extravagant practice of sports and games, this cult, this adulation of the body, this voluntarily restricted horizon, this intransigence, this lack of tolerance in the manifestations of social life, these concessions to nothing but well-being and personal comfort, this lack of humanity, these narrow prejudices and this complicated ceremonial which lays down the different degrees of worthiness of human beings, this situation of a group of people at the ends of the earth, this voluntary insularity, exclusive and individual, this optimism à deux, this mutual admiration in the bosom of the family, this complaisance in the face of everything concerning love, this communal salacity, this erotic curiosity which affects the young people very early and which still shakes couples in their extreme old age, this self-satisfaction, this pride, this arrogance, this selectivity, this refusal to cross-breed, this fine health of the body – in brief, all that the New Zealander of today considers to be his conquest and his achievement, the manifest signs of his independence from old Europe, and even this independence itself . . . when one looks at all this close to, making allowances for a certain materialistic aspect that modern life tends to take on more and more in every region of the globe, and especially in the most far-flung places, where this contemporary trend towards uniformity and massiveness is increasing day by day, one perceives that nothing has changed in these islands, that New Zealand has made no progress at all, and that life continues as in the time of the cannibals and expresses itself through a whole series of laws, interdictions, repressions and cruel dreams under the aegis of the great god Taboo. The idyllic life of the New Zealanders, like that of the aborigines, is savage, with this sole difference: nowadays, in the pastures fenced in by barbed wire, they fatten up cattle, whereas, once upon a time, in the huts made of bamboo canes, they fattened up men, choice victims destined for the tribal feasts of human flesh. The only thing lacking to make the parallel perfect is that the New Zealanders have not yet had occasion to make war on each other, a fratricidal war. However, I fought with them during the war and it is true that they showed themselves to be good soldiers.

At the front, I thought about all these things as I gazed out of my loophole. I had just returned from a patrol. The dawn was slow in coming. The flares were diminishing. Our line was silent, but the one opposite us was blasting away; the Germans started their ranging fire on our trenches early. All our men were still asleep. The trench was deserted. I gazed out at the barbed wire, at the *chevaux de frise*, at no man's land, searching for a zig zag trench amongst the enemy barbed-wire entanglements, while still dreaming of those vast empty countries I knew in different parts of the world, countries where the interior is still uninhabited and belongs, for the most part, to no one, yet is already divided by networks of barbed-wire fences. How, in those lost wildernesses, the chattering of the wild duck and the water-fowl made my heart beat faster! Colonel Butcher never woke up till very late. While waiting to report, I preferred to lie in wait for the dawn in front of an abandoned loophole rather than go into the dug-outs and watch my comrades sleeping.

. . . .

My most frightening memories of the war are of those nights I was compelled to spend in a bomb-proof shelter watching my comrades sleep. One man is sprawled on his back, another on his stomach, some are curled up, others are lying with arms, legs, trousers agape, some snore, others whine and whimper as if tormented by worms, some wake up to eat, others to go out and urinate, one clenches his fists and cries out in his dreams, another is having a fight with himself, another is struggling as if caught in a spider's web, still another is silently biting his tongue. They are all grimacing, all tossing and turning, lying in tortured and ungainly postures. Limbs flung out, jaws slack, faces full of shadowy holes, and the skin of the belly, the back or the chest glistening in puddles of sweaty nudity. They look like abortions, a swarm of half-formed beings, heads attached to legs and buttocks to shoulders, ectoplasm materializing in the light of a flickering candle, which the blast from the explosions outside keeps extinguishing, so that I have to keep relighting it. The litter of weapons scattered in the verminous straw, of haversacks and packs spilling out into the mud, bits of clothing, rags, unravelled bandages floating in the oozing water, add an indescribably macabre confusion to the spectacle of their sleep.

I closed my eyes.

In the terrifying silence between two explosions I could hear the distant breathing of my comrades rising from the depths of their beings, racing in their chests, roaring as it drew near, increasing in volume as it whistled before bursting out of their mouths in the form of raucous coughs, lugubrious snorts, hiccups and sighs like the shells which burst out of the mouths of field-guns to fall on our heads, shells which came from a long way off and often hovered for a moment with a strange yawning sound. I had the feeling that, at some time in my life, I had already recorded that extraordinary symphony, in which the most furious detonations were no louder than a suffocated wail, and the secret groan of an anguished heart overwhelmed the voice of the field-guns. Listening to all this resounding in the depths of my being, my head spun and, insensibly, I began to evoke those long winter nights in the hut on Sturge Island, when the blizzard raged outside and I made a noise, as much noise as possible, starting up all my phonographs and all my gramophones so as not to hear the groaning of my silent comrades, which dominated the cosmic racket of the tempest. It was my way of defending myself, for I want to live! Arkadie Goischman, André Lamont, and you, little Ivan, what did you want from me? Today, I still do not share your sufferings, any more than, at the time, I understood your agonies and your dreams, nor why you died impotently, even though you wanted to live your lives.

I shook myself.

I could no longer breathe in the stuffy hut.

Without the slightest hesitation or any misgivings I went out.

Outside, the storm was at its height, raging with the violence of Armageddon. If I am to be killed, so be it, but I want to live.

I staggered, bent double and tacking between the fierce gusts and the showers of earth and stones flung by the whirlwind. I made slow progress. The ground gave way beneath me. I heard cries, calls, moans. The crater-riddled field started to whirl round madly and it seemed to me that a flashing sword, flinging off roaring sparks, fell from the heavens to smite and massacre everything on the surface of the earth, like a gramophone needle scratching, scoring, digging furrows in an old, already worn record, on a fully-wound gramophone, whose human voices are finally and irrevocably doomed.

. . . .

It is night. It's raining. I look out. Darkness. Not a sound. I talk to myself. My voice annoys me. I put my dictaphone on my knees and speak into it very, very quietly, as if whispering into its ear.

Listen, are the intonations of the wind always the same? Does the sea that breaks on the basalt rocks of Cape Tasman roar like the ocean that breaks on the coasts of America or beats against the white cliffs of Dover?

What is happening tonight?

The fact is, I am haunted by the memory of so many sleepless nights, in different latitudes, indoors or out under the stars, that even here I am still on the watch.

There is something in the air that troubles me.

I often open my door.

If I were a bird, I should fly away.

The melted snow that spins and eddies, the rain falling in cataracts and the wind that guffaws, flattens itself, then blows in gusts in all directions, are so many harbingers of spring. It can't last much longer. Spring is coming. I am not mistaken. Although it has not yet reached this valley, it is already prowling across the plains. It is on these heavily overcast nights that, at sea, one hears the passing of invisible flocks of migratory birds, very high in the black sky.

In the Falklands, which are devoid of hills and trees, the spring storm has a single unvarying rhythm and rushes through space like an express train, disturbing the penguins and making them cry, day and night, as if there had been a catastrophe, while in Brazil the spring winds emerge mysteriously from the depths of the virgin forests that surround the bay of Santa Catarina to wander over the waves and mingle with the breath of the manatees and the sperm whales.

In Chile, in the Gulf of Talcahuano, you hear the wailing of the seals of La Quirine, the eddies of the Mocha and the call of the great nocturnal birds of prey which are flocking together for the seasonal pairing.

What an infinity of love-songs, melodies, voices, in the infinite variety of birds!

In Chiloé, in the San Carlos hills, the birds sang me marvellous rhapsodies. Their singing would last a good two hours then stop, always at the same moment, just as day was breaking. The white-throated tree runner, the bird the natives call the *toui-toui*, then emits thousands of rapid roulades, fluent, trilling and sonorous, which he scatters like beads, and the *kaou-kaou-pâ*, the big dove, coos like a double bass, while the sea-pie, the mocking-bird and the Nestor parrot exult and the bell-bird utters his tin-tin-tin, which sounds like a triangle.

Last spring, at Saint-Gervais, I watched the flight of the eagles. There was a pair of them nesting in a rocky cliff, to the left, above the Platé desert. I had sighted their eyrie through the field-glasses and every day I promised myself I would go and dislodge them, for the spring was already well advanced . . .

Yes, the spring was already well advanced, for there were a great many deaths among the patients in the sanatorium where Mireille was dying; all the invalids who had survived the winter were being carried off, they could not withstand the spring. I was in a hurry to get away.

'Let it end soon, let me get away!' I said to myself. 'Poor Mireille!'

It made me dizzy.

I got a crick in the neck from watching the gliding flight of the eagles, which described circles in the empty sky, turning and turning within the range of my field-glasses. Everything would start to swing round me, as on those nights at sea when you lie flat on your back on the ship's deck, following the truck of the mainmast with your eyes as it describes circles amongst the stars; in the end, it seems as if the sky itself is swaying and the stars moving, making you feverish, blind, as the stars come to perch on you, fly away again, return once more to hum in your ears like those swarms of imaginary flies that torment a dying man, whose terrified gaze is already peering into the tomb but whose pupils stray, unseeing, over the ceiling. There is something prodigious about silence. I was so far away yet so close to it all, so calm and so anxious, and I made such efforts to follow the eagles with my field-glasses, so as to throw the nurses off the scent as they passed along the corridor behind me; so far away and yet so close that I could hear all the sounds coming from Mireille's room, a spoon stirring something in a glass, the clink of a jug, a slight rattle of china, but not the doctor opening the door of that room in front of which I had been stationed since dawn, awaiting his verdict, nor the words he addressed to me.

Every morning he had to shake me by the shoulder.

It was then eleven o'clock. I still had time to escape to the mountain.

'Well, doctor?'

The doctor was glum.

'Any change?'

'Nothing.'

'No improvement?'

'No.'

I left, juggling with my field-glasses.

On the mountain I was free. On the mountain I was alone.

I could breathe.

I rolled in the grass. I slept under the pines. I went and sat on a rock.

The sky was empty.

I looked for my eagles.

Through my field-glasses I studied the mountain facing me.

One day I shall climb up there.

After . . . after the funeral . . . I shall buy a double-barrelled gun
. . . I shall kill them.

.   .   .   .

Cylinder Seven

. . . .

The Plan de l'Aiguille, 21st April 1925 (continued)
I was free. I was alone. I could breathe.

At the front, too, I used to follow my instinct, wandering all night long in a state of madness.

What a strange cacophony! I could hear death raving in delirium. An anonymous piece of machinery!

But by concentrating hard, I managed to subdue my nerves. In the end I was able to make out a series of little notes which I couldn't get out of my head; they were tirelessly repeated, monotonously persistent and continued to assert themselves discreetly, softly, with the regularity of a beating pulse, even in the midst of the tumult.

Was it the beating of my heart? No.

After this last failure to identify the sound, I managed to get my bearings.

It rang out freely. It consisted of little cries, weak, spaced out, too faint to drown the clamour of the guns.

The voices of the past? The present? The future?

I pin-pointed the direction from which it was coming.

At that time we were on the Somme.

It was coming from the water.

I slipped through the marshes like a water-rat, for I knew the area like the back of my hand. I plunged in among the reeds. I came upon an old hunters' hide, abandoned since the beginning of the war. I went in, lay down and stretched out. I kept quite still. Life was there, behind a wattle screen. I could hear it chattering, cackling, laughing. Ducks, water-fowl, grebes, snipe, plovers and rails were innocently playing there. I pulled back the wattle screen. There was no one but me to see them. The night was drawing to a close. I was alive. I was breathing. Ah!

. . . .

I also remember a bird that let out a single, solitary cry, like a creaking see-saw. No one has ever been able to tell me its name. I saw it sometimes down on the marshes; it flew so low that the tips of its wings rippled the water. It was a swift, fleeting bird, shaped like a sickle. It zigzagged, skimmed the ground and, like a boomerang, always came back to the same spot; no sooner had it perched somewhere than it let out its badly oiled cry. It was a brownish bird, handsomely shaped.

I used to think about that bird while listening distractedly to the suggestions of my fellow-debauchees.

Big Kugelhopf was there, a Swiss engineer who had made an immense fortune selling rotten sleepers for the construction of the Trans-Siberian railway; Susuce, a lieutenant in the Guards, whom the women still nicknamed 'The Prince Corset' or 'Handsome Oscar'; the Pantaleon brothers, bankers, who were better known on the Stock Exchange as 'The Dirty Shirts'; the Mad Virgin, an ether addict; Miss Wee-Wee, a tearful old horsewoman, always hacking and coughing; two or three young Hungarian girls, who were just starting on a life of debauchery and hadn't yet acquired nicknames; me, known in town as 'The Lucky Devil' because of my trotters, which won all the races, and, amongst intimate friends, as 'The King of Bluff' because of the fishing licences I had obtained from the Imperial Government. (Amongst themselves the theatre girls called me 'A Thousand Pounds and One Night' because of the fee I paid them for their favours, and because I never felt like spending more than one night with any of them.) . . .

It must have been one of our first parties, because once again it was spring, that bitter-sweet spring you get in St Petersburg, which smells of dust, ammonia, horse-dung and, on the Islands, of

birch trees, rushes and bilberries, then suddenly, when you get out
of the carriage to go into the Cubas Brothers' famous restaurant,
of gypsies and grease-paint, and of French cuisine, which kindles
women's laughter and makes them sparkle.

Ah, that springtime in St Petersburg!

Ah, that first laughter of women in the open air, the kisses
exchanged, the greedy caresses, those lavish suppers in the
flickering dusk, full of the promise of spring, that carnal appetite,
that physical intoxication, that palpable happiness of the body,
that sensual swoon at table! One experiences this only in northern
countries, in the spring!

'In love, the only thing that changes is the colour of the silk
stockings. As for women, it's *toujours la même chose*.'

Who had uttered this inane remark? I never knew, for, just as I
was about to protest, a woman came and planted herself in front
of me.

Where had she sprung from? She was tall and aggressive and
seemed very worked up about something. Had she heard that
hollow phrase one of us had just uttered? I don't know. Anyway,
there she was, planted in front of me.

'Idiot!' she cried, following up this insult with a typical Russian
curse. 'Idiot! Look at me!'

And she suddenly flung open her fur coat. Underneath it she
was stark naked.

What a milestone in my life!

Next day I fought duels with young Gargarine, the man she
really loved, and with Prince Michael Tamamcheff, her protector,
who was the finest swordsman in the garrison.

Much later, Hedwiga - for it was Hedwiga! - confessed to me
that the whole absurd incident was the result of a challenge. Her
own circle of friends didn't believe her capable of creating such a
scandal, so she had made a bet that she would give herself,
publicly, to me. Alas! At the time Hedwiga did not know she
would fall in love. And nor did I. . . .

I can still hear the cry of that bird whose name I never knew, and
I still wonder who could have uttered that idiotic phrase about
women and love, a phrase which is engraved on my brain and
which, today, seems to me the most profound truth ever spoken

concerning the society of the now defunct St Petersburg, a society which could so easily be dismissed as frivolous but was in fact deeply and intensely thrilling.

I have inquired into the subject. Not one of the people who were at table with me on the night I met Hedwiga remembers this phrase. No one else heard it. I have always suspected Kugelhopf of having said it, but he too swears he knows nothing about it; however, it was very much in his style as a compulsive Don Juan, and matched his cold and cynical spirit. When I spoke to him about it, he asked me to repeat it, jotted it down in his notebook and said: 'My dear friend, you will never convince me that you didn't invent those words yourself!'

And he left me, gargling the phrase over and over, as if he wanted to learn it by heart and recite it to everyone he met. What an ass!

I saw Kugelhopf again last year. He was passing through Paris on his way to embark for New York, where he was to launch and finance the giant Sirosky aeroplanes. It was from him that, at last, I had news of Hedwiga.

'Princess Hedwiga', he told me, 'suffered more than anyone else during the Russian Revolution. They say that, in terror of the revolutionaries, she had shut herself up in a pigsty, and she let herself be eaten alive by a starving sow rather than call for help.'

'But . . . but her husband?' I asked, horrified.

'The Prince? The Prince had just been appointed Viceroy of the Caucasus. He was one of the Bolsheviks' first victims . . .'

'And . . . and . . . her child?'

'Her son, little Nicholas? He is reported missing.'

Kugelhopf was full of swank at being able to give me these details. He himself had managed to escape in time, via Finland. He had become enormously fat. His face was devoured by erysipelas. He told me a few more anecdotes about my old boozing pals, all of whom had been caught up, more or less tragically, in the events.

'You understand, my dear friend, the war, the Revolution. There's nothing left. I think we are the last two survivors of that happy crew of *bons viveurs*. You . . . you were always known as "The Lucky Devil", but for an old rascal like me, what is left?

What will become of me, do you think? I'm no longer fit for anything but to work myself to death in aviation.'

And Kugelhopf left me, humming an operatic aria.

. . . .

At Cambrai, my nocturnal promenades amongst the shattered tanks and the smoking ruins, under heavy gunfire, had already begun to draw attention to myself, and now that I was spending whole mornings in the marshes, I acquired a reputation for bravery.

It was not long before the men I was with unanimously chose me to organize and lead patrols, and Colonel Butcher gave me *carte blanche* as to selecting the men and the objectives.

The French army was moving slowly to the right; the English army, which had been holed up in billets further north, had now come to dig in on the Somme. The New Zealanders were therefore sent down from Cambrai and Bapaume to relieve the French in the Friesland salient, and it was the Anzac Corps, to which I belonged, which occupied the outermost point of the salient. This point was extremely vulnerable, for it was the hinge of the immense pincer, one branch of which extended as far as the North Sea and the other as far as the Swiss frontier. Moreover, this sector was subjected to an intense bombardment. To be accurate, there were no longer any trenches on either side, because this hinge was well and truly in the marshes. Liaison from one bank to the other was established at night by patrols. Three English patrols came over every night from Hurlu, and six Anzac patrols set out every night from La Grenouillère. The Germans sent as many from their side and this led, several times a night, to exciting encounters, furious skirmishes with side-arms, ambushes and raids which were carried out from boats or by swimming. It was a partisans' guerrilla warfare, a kind of independent little war within the big one, and you had to be alert, cunning, wily, resourceful, quick, not to mention daring to the point of madness, to surprise an enemy patrol or take a few prisoners, often well behind the lines.

And so, every night, all this immense war effort, which had the entire world on tenterhooks, depended on a handful of men who paddled about in the water, lost their footing in the bogs and, if they managed to accomplish their mission, did so blindly, groping

97

in the dark and the wet. Like the generalissimo, lost in his reveries or poring over difficult calculations as to the probabilities, I have often felt the whole weight of the war resting on my shoulders, with just this difference: while the generalissimo stayed comfortably at his fireside, I was at the mercy of the wind, water and darkness, lost in the fog, floundering in the mud, holding my breath before lighting a flare, getting scorched by bullets, bursting into little outposts, grabbing a sentry with my bare hands, throwing bombs, firing my Parabellum, escaping, nine times out of ten, by swimming, carrying equipment, documents or a live man, whom I was holding by the throat.

However, those of us who belonged to the patrol did have other vital compensations, which the generalissimo probably knew nothing about: we drew a quintuple rum ration and were given lots of extra leave. Naturally our leave passes were valid for Paris.

I can say, and not without pride, that I never lost a man on any of these patrols. Moreover, ever since my arrival at the front, I had been considered as a kind of mascot, a lucky charm in my company: the men squabbled over who was to be in my patrol, and in fact going out with me was known as 'going to Paris', 'going to Montmartre', or 'going on the binge', so sure were they that they'd come back safe and sound.

'Right, let's go and get our passes for Paris. Tonight we'll take them off the Boches!' they would say.

And they would crawl out, giving each other the password: *Nach Paris!*

. . . .

The Admiralties of Great Britain, France, Italy and Japan were at their wits' end over an elusive enemy who was never to be seen, but whose existence was signalled everywhere as a menace to the Australian convoys.

Dozens of torpedo-boats, squadrons of armour-plated ships and even fleets of Dreadnoughts were alerted to give chase to this phantom enemy, which was variously reported to be, now the *Königsberg*, the *Dresden*, the *Scharnhorst* or the *Emden*, now Admiral von Spee's fleet of armour-plated cruisers, whose vessels had sailed to the Falklands shortly after I embarked, and some of which had forged on into the extreme northern extremities of my fishing concession, to Port Deception. (And I may as well admit here and now that, when Dr Schmoll and his crew disembarked on my island, they came as emissaries of the German navy, and, specifically, to prepare a base for this very fleet.) When I embarked on the *Worcestershire*, in Wellington, there were rumours that new privateers were scouring the Indian Ocean, and one of them, probably the *Wolf*, had been detached to lay a minefield directly in front of Wellington!

Nobody wanted to believe this fantastic story, but nevertheless they took every possible precaution with our precious convoy. All sorts of ruses were employed: false news bulletins, false departures, to keep the route secret. We wasted time, traversing thousands of miles of ocean off course. We advanced, retreated, looped back on ourselves, broke down, got lost, joined up again, took on coal during a storm, performed the most absurd evolutions and drove the General Staff crazy.

And so the heavy Australian troopships navigated blindly, mutely, went aground, tacked one after the other into the sounds, played hide-and-seek amongst the islands, flocked together unexpectedly, far out at sea, and sailed in convoy well outside the normal navigation lanes.

Ingenuity was stretched to breaking-point.

Every day, submarines, picket-boats, trawlers and aeroplanes appeared in zones which had never yet heard the sound of an internal combustion engine. Day and night, without a second's pause, telegraphy, espionage and the Intelligence service cast their nets ever more tightly over the immense desert of the waters. No snippet of information was ignored, every little sign was taken into account. Millions were spent to keep this unheard-of method of navigation up to the mark, in order to safeguard this reinforcement of men, of enthusiastic patriotism, of equipment, which was all arriving from overseas under camouflage, for the services responsible for them had calculated everything in advance and were relying on the surprise effect of the sudden apparition of these fresh forces in the various theatres of war in the West.

The men themselves were totally uninterested in this gigantic game of chess that was being played on the surface of three oceans, even though their own safety and their very lives were at stake. I have seen them laugh when danger was announced, shrug their shoulders when they were warned about enemy privateers and sneer at the threat of torpedoes. But I have also seen them charge the rail and lean over, craning their necks, every man jack of them on the same side, to the point where the ship took on a list, when they heard that land was in sight.

Each and every man was in thrall to his own fantasies, they were all dreaming of women, writing to women, conjuring up women, talking about women, imagining women, waiting for women, hoping for women, preparing to enjoy women. There would be new ones, new women at every port of call! And they deserved them all!

But what bitter disillusionment – everywhere they were kept in quarantine!

We passed far out, always far out to sea.

Of the islands we glimpsed, the towns, the ports, the tufts of gently swaying palms, the pointed roofs of pagodas, the fretwork bazaars, the songs, the music, the gesticulations, the native silhouettes on the shore, the inviting calls from the quay or the bottom of small boats, the hot effluvia of the night, the laughter, nothing remains, not a memory, not a single kiss. However, in accordance with Napoleon's axiom that an army marches on its stomach, the troops' rations were good, abundant and varied, and fresh food was taken on at each port of call (where oranges, lemons, pineapples, mangoes, water-melons, avocados and bananas, lots of bananas, were given out), but where is the great modern general who, alone amongst all the experts, the specialists and the wise men, who concern themselves with a million details, would have the audacity and the genius to think humbly of his men's lower abdomens? The few soldiers who managed to slip ashore were hustled back on board with blows of the rubber truncheon, and they came back sad, dazed, defeated, dead drunk, shamefaced and still more unsatisfied than those who had remained on board.

If, as the seasonal migrations of birds and fish, and certain instinctual phenomena among insects would lead one to believe, sexual irritation is a fluid that emits radiations of a physical order which propagate through space with the concordance of the waves in a disturbed atmosphere, was it not inevitable that, during the course of this voyage (just as, in an electric circuit under the influence of a magnet, the currents physicists call 'induced circuits' are produced) the desires, the fantasies, the dreams of all these young males, isolated on the high seas, must heat up to such a point as to change their very nature and frequency, thus causing sexual disorientation and erotic exacerbation?

I have witnessed this debauch of the imagination which was, properly speaking, a massive assuagement, made universal through telepathy. (I believe it is in this area that we must seek the cause of the general derangement of morals which has been observed throughout the entire world since the war.)

The convoy put in a sudden appearance in Colombo, loaded munitions in Bombay, hid itself in the sound of Bab-el-Mandab, split up to take on coal quickly at Aden or Djibouti, and discharged its cargo of men and beasts, helter-skelter, in Arabia, in the Sinai and in Egypt.

So we were on dry land, but life there was just as untenable as it had been on board.

We had to drill in the camps and out in the desert. We were made to march in columns of four in the sand and the dust, work our way right through King's Regulations to inculcate the external marks of respect into our very souls, but I have seen men weep with frenzy and desire on the banks of the Suez Canal, where they made us dig trenches.

After this purgatory in the sand, it was hell amongst the stones, the last stage before we arrived in France.

They made us build terraces and concrete emplacements for the heavy batteries under fire from the forts, and I have seen men go mad with rage and mad with love in the furnace of Gallipoli.

What did they care about the Turks? It was women, women, women they needed!

At night, in our tents, they talked of nothing else, and they were still talking about women at dawn, beneath the fading stars, when the shadows were stealing out under the barbed wire of the camp, to disappear and couple in some remote gully.

The soldiers were not coenobites, or anchorites, or saints. They had taken no vows. They dreamed. They languished. Out of boredom, they had themselves tattooed. Each man had his own particular bee in his bonnet. One morning I surprised a man who was tossing himself off between two stones. There was not a dot on the horizon, not even a sail on the sea. The sun was merciless. There was plenty of blood spilled at Gallipoli, but the soil was watered still more with sperm. The entire army ejaculated there, and the seed was spilled as uselessly as the blood. Our soldiers had names tattooed on their skins - *Marie, Louise, Sarah, Rose* - but it is at Gallipoli that you will find the tomb of the Unknown Woman, in the midst of their anonymous graves.

Oh, Paris! Once we abandoned Gallipoli, all the desires of the survivors were focused on you! . . . .

. . . .

. . . . PARIS . . . .

. . . . PARIS . . . .

. . . . . . PARIS . . . .

PARIS . . . .

. . . . PARIS . . . .

. . . . PARIS . . . .

. . . . PARIS

. . . .

. . . .

Cylinder Eight

I have left the chalet on the Plan. I am going back to Paris. I have made up my mind. I'm beginning to get fed up. What with, I don't know. Everything. Nothing. I am bored.

Today is 11th June. It is the anniversary of Mireille's death. It is. . . . Ah! Why does everything repeat itself, and yet nothing comes back to you? . . . Like last year, I climb up into the larch forest, I climb up to Le Prarion and lie down in the grass.

The pastures are superb. The spring flowers are blooming in clusters. There are still patches of snow in the hollows and under the last pine trees. The slate quarries on the col de Voza are full of water. There are swarms of little butterflies, bumble-bees and drones. When I move, because the ants are disturbing me, I hear marmots whistling in the dell at Tricot. The gentians and hoarhound intoxicate me. I fall alseep. It is midday.

Sleep, when it comes to me, is perhaps the best chance I have to live! Nevertheless, when I wake up at about three o'clock, I am in a gloomy mood.

Then, so as not to have to go down again immediately, I push on as far as Mont Lachat, following the cutting of the little tramway from Mont Blanc. I march along, balancing on the rail, or taking giant strides so as not to miss the sleepers. I count my steps. I am bored. I whistle. I swing my cane. I beat time. I stop to light my pipe.

The little station at Mont Lachat is still buried in the snow, only the stove-pipe is sticking out. Perhaps there's somebody down there, somebody who is watching me as one watches an enemy through a periscope? I shout down the stove-pipe 'Hey, you down there, coffee's up!' and run away. Nothing stirs.

I climb a little higher, on the slope of the Rognes, the rotten mountain, and, hauling myself up on to a rock, I look down over the valley of Chamonix.

I gaze at it for the last time.

How it has changed since last winter! How hollowed out it looks, how wrinkled and pleated, and how swollen the slopes have become! The valley is stretched out in front of me, split like an open vulva between the peaks that surround it and the lewd, glittering summits that dominate it and rise vertiginously into the air. The long flows of white firn, the trails of glaciers stagnate amongst the sombre green pines that are massed together, tufted and dense as fur.

Why does this view make me sad?

I turn my back on it.

I go away, feeling melancholy.

I go back down via Motivon, still following the tramlines.

Half-way down, I bump into Pierre, the porter from Tête-Rousse. He's sleeping off his wine. He has put down his load and is lying on the tram-tracks.

I give him a shake.

'Hey, Pierre! Pierre, wake up, you'll get run over!'

He grunts.

'Come on, get up, you old swine, we'll go and have a jar together!'

I have a sudden, mad desire to go and get drunk with this brute in whose company, last year, I did the rounds of all the bars in Fayet.

'Pierre, come and have a drink!'

I help him to his feet.

'Ah! . . . It's you, boss. . . . Cheers, bottoms up, at y'service!' he says, recovering his equilibrium. 'V'happy to see you . . . v'happy. . . .'

I pick up his pack, grab his arm and we go up the slope again.

'Ah!' he says. 'I'm v'happy to see you, I was jist c'min' t'see you! Come this way. . . .'

And, taking a little path that runs steeply down into a ravine, he adds: 'Th'people in Saint-Gervais, th're all cunts, as y'might say. Us two, us two'll go down to Bionnassay. Th'boys there've got more balls, we'll have a good old punch-up, and they've got some decent booze, y'know. All communists down there, a proud commune . . . well, you'll see f'yourself, huh? No, honest, boss, I'm pleased t'see you!'

I spent the night with Pierre. We drank all night long. I drank all night long without managing to get drunk. That, too, is over. It's time I left.

Today I sent Pierre to look for Lucienne at Saint-Nicolas-de-Véroce, telling him to bring her back to me, whatever the cost. Now I am in my room, the same room I had last year; they thought I'd be pleased to have the same one, No. 17. When I get to Paris, I shall move house. I am once more in the hotel at Mont Joly and, like last year, I've got a bottle of whisky on the table and I'm pacing up and down my room.

Why, I wonder, did I send this telegram:

ESSOR-AUTO 7 RUE DU RANELAGH PARIS. SEND ME BY ROAD THE FASTEST CAR YOU HAVE IN STOCK STOP CORDIALLY DAN YACK MONTJOLY SAINT-GERVAIS HAUTE-SAVOIE.

And I wonder what my friend What's-his-name . . . (fancy that, I've forgotten his name) will send me?

. . . .

Last time I went to Paris it was in a 3-litre Alfa Romeo which could do 140 kilometres an hour, with ease. There was not a moment to lose. I drove across the whole of France like a madman and was lucky enough to arrive in time to find Max Hyène at his desk in the rue du Helder.

Why hadn't I consulted him before? He could have given me good advice. If there was still some avenue to be explored, he would have pointed it out to me. Max is never fooled by words. He knows everything. He knows everybody. And who knows whether the story about his wife is true?

Mireille had been given up by the doctors. Things were very bad. A famous professor had just left, after letting fall the words 'pithiatic coprostasis'. As soon as I found out what it meant, the name of Max Hyène came to my mind. Didn't his wife suffer from a similar malady, which Max enjoyed making jokes about after dinner? He always managed to astonish his guests by relating the story:

'Do you know that Mme Max Hyène and I have been sleeping in separate rooms for more than forty years? And do you know why? Ah, well! because Mme Max Hyène, my dear, does poopoo into a pair of scales!'

'Precision scales,' he hastens to add.

And, seeing the horror on his guest's face, Max repeats: 'As I have had the honour of telling you, my dear friend, into a pair of scales!'

And he continues his bantering: 'To tell you the whole truth, I am forced to admit that Mme Max Hyène is of too delicate a nature to do things like other people . . . a pair of precision scales is not enough, she must also have her doctor in attendance.'

And, as he gets carried away: 'She does it with her doctor, as if she were cuckolding me with the priest at confession!'

And, solemnly: 'But I don't hold with it at all – I'm an old rascal, an old pagan, what is called a free-thinker, you know. My generation is all for science, we no longer bow down before the priests but before the doctor!'

Artfully: 'Diseases of this sort are, like religious bigotry, affectations adopted by women to annoy their husbands. . . . Ah, don't ever get married, my young friend,' he advises now, pathetic and good-natured.

Then, vulgarly: 'It's a good joke, and I pretend to take Madame's comedy seriously.'

In a businesslike tone: 'I must have the figures!'

Like a crafty schoolboy: 'Every morning I open the door of Mme Max Hyène's room a little way and ask: "How much, Amélie?" "A sixth, my dear", or "A seventh, my dear", or "A ninth", replies the hypocrite, smirking on her scales. "Well, take care of yourself, my dearest!" and off I go to the office, rubbing my hands.'

At this point in his recital Max is very cheerful. He usually offers you a cigar, pours you a glass of brandy and asks, jubilantly: 'You know what those figures mean . . . a sixth, a seventh, a ninth?'

And, in the face of his guest's ignorance, he intones pompously: 'A healthy subject, following a normal dietary regime, evacuates a quantity of matter equal to one-eighth of the food ingested during the same twenty-four hours.'

And, suddenly confidential: 'This morning Madame did one-seventh!'

Solemnly: 'That's why we have not had the pleasure of her company at dinner.'

As a perfect man-of-the-world: 'Mme Max Hyène is unwell, she has asked me to apologize for her absence.'

Familiarly: 'Her rules of hygiene, you understand, oblige her to use the scales when she eats, as well.'

And, roaring with laughter: 'Don't worry, it's not the same pair! Engineering comes in useful, it was I who worked out these figures and made her a present of the second pair of scales,' he adds, choking with laughter.

Finally, taking you aside, he concludes: 'Don't you think, my dear, that I've managed to get my own back on that doctor?'

When I arrived in the rue du Helder, Max's office was packed as always after Stock Exchange hours with an amiable crowd of chorus girls, actors, the racing fraternity, snobs, tenors, baritones and, above all, female Wagnerian singers and concert artistes because the great passion of Max's entire life has been to discover and launch these musical women.

Max's friends represented a whole epoch that was coming to an end, and it was Max who had been its chief instigator and its kingpin. When he dies, it will all collapse. I cannot imagine the Paris of the *bons viveurs* without Max Hyène's table, without Max's dinners, Max's wine-cellar, Max's cigars, Max's girl-friends, Max's concerts and his operas, without Max's stories, his *coups*, the deals he pulls off on the Stock Exchange, his top hats, his inside information and his fiddles, which he turns largely to the profit of his whole entourage of friends, mistresses and *protégées*.

Today Max Hyène is eighty-two years old. He is an enormous old man, all bloated and swollen up. He is so corpulent he couldn't get through the template of a railway engine. One is always afraid he will burst out of his clothes, or that his armchair will collapse under his weight, or his desk give way when he is sitting on it. If it weren't for the chronic cataracts eating away at both his eyes, compelling him to wear a whole range of ever more complicated lenses, you wouldn't think he was so old. He is still ferociously active. Seeing him moving, swaggering about, laughing, carrying on ten conversations at once, challenging everybody, singing an aria, telling outrageous stories, paying an old ogre's compliments to some shy young débutante, you realize why this man needed to ransack the five continents in order to satisfy the cravings of his temperament and the entrepreneurial bent of his intelligence. All the good restaurants in the world have heard his laugh and admired his magisterial palate and his hearty appetite; a good many dishes have been named after him; but he was also able to conquer the Alps, penetrate the Andes, bestride Niagara, bring life to the centre of Australia and Asia, even lost Chaco, by giving them railways with a daily service, and to bring Baghdad within three days' reach of Berlin and build his masterpiece, that wildly daring line that loops the loop and climbs right up into the extreme north of Canada, a line on which, once a week, there is a luxury train which is the last word in comfort and modern technology. Max Hyène is surely the greatest engineer of the nineteenth century.

I must say now that I feel quite at home in his house, for Max was my father's most faithful friend and his partner at baccarat. They had innumerable adventures together, shared the same mistresses, the same horses, the same speculative gambles, and, when I wanted to build my factory, it was Max Hyène whom I consulted about the plans. Max is very fond of me and has always received me with kindness and indulgence. And I don't have to stand on ceremony with him, especially since he was a witness at my wedding. In spite of all this, I did not know how to broach the subject and talk to him about the very thing I had come for.

How could I tell him that Mireille was dying? Explain that she refused to eat, drink or evacuate? How could I tell him they were torturing her and she no longer wanted to see me? Tell him that, for months and months, she had been struggling in the grip of a horrible nightmare, and would cry out, weep the whole night long, and then suddenly, during the day, start shouting: 'I don't want to! I don't want to!' And that at other times she would spend weeks quietly sitting up in bed saying 'No, no, no!' and shaking her head? How could I tell him that she seemed to have forgotten me, but that she had acute fits of anxiety when she called me by name, murmuring the tenderest endearments, so that they had to come running to fetch me and, when I arrived, she didn't recognize me, stubbornly refused to speak, repulsed me, became agitated, restless, furious, frantically tearing at her night-dress, starting to shake her head again – 'No, no, no! – and twisting her arms in rage and despair? How could I tell him that she wanted to disfigure herself and that they were threatening her with a straitjacket? How could I tell him all that?

I felt like going away without a word, but I didn't. I said to myself: 'Perhaps Max can cure her, he is sure to know of a similar case. With his vast experience of women, and of life, he will be able to tell me what to do. He will fish an address out of his prodigious memory, an address or the name of a specialist, a doctor, a surgeon, an alienist, a homoeopath, a masseur, a hypnotist, a vitalist, a charlatan, a healer, perhaps a priest, who will be able to do something for Mireille. He has no prejudices and he knows everybody, including quacks!'

As his office showed no signs of emptying, and all these beautiful people were busy gossiping, chattering, scandalmongering, flirting, smiling, smoking and drinking, each trying to outdo the others, I saw that I would have to wait some time before I could put myself in Max's hands, so I pretended to be interested in the drawings and photographs on the walls. There were sectional drawings of the latest models of railway engines, Pullman cars, cranes and snow-ploughs. There was a photograph of a bridge built entirely of iron which, in a single span, crossed a dried-out river in an arid desert bristling with candelabra cactus and tufts of alfa grass with thick prickles. It must have been somewhere in Arizona or Colorado. Framed under glass were some little yellowed and mildewed Kodak snaps taken at God knows what work-site in South Africa. They showed Negroes, naked or dressed in cast-offs, dancing in front of a row of tip-wagons standing on a railway line in the process of construction, or standing in heraldic poses around a giant excavator, or singing as they worked a concrete-mixer or a crushing-roller mounted on rails. A gang of workers, shirtless but with their leather hats armed with acetylene lamps, posed for the photographer in the gallery of a tunnel. Max Hyène himself must have taken the photograph, because all the men were smiling. The monstrous tubes of pneumatic drills were wound all round their naked torsos like the wires and flexes of an electric tattooing machine. Elsewhere there was a diver directing the placing of piles, a crew of firemen installing a turntable and a flag-bedecked demilune under the falling snow in a mountainous landscape, and some immense scaffolding in the shape of a filigree 'Z' reaching up to the level of . . .

I repeated to myself: 'Perhaps Max, who knows so many recipes, will recall some concoction or folk remedy, a balm, a powder, a vermifuge, a root, an unguent, an American herb tea, a water, an emetic, a formula to recite, a ritual gesture, an incantation or a prayer. It is not possible that a man who can resolve so many complex problems, who can create works of public utility, transform life on the surface of this globe, bring well-being to hitherto benighted regions, instil habits of hygiene and comfort into isolated tribesmen and give them electric light, it is not possible that this man should be unable to get me out of this mess!' Then I began to doubt: 'After all, one never knows, perhaps Mme Hyène is really ill, suffering from a nervous disorder of the same kind as Mireille's, or some inexplicable mental derangement, and she drags on year after year, and Max is powerless to bring her any relief, and so he's desperate, and all the cynicism he displays with so much complacency is nothing but a mask to hide his love? Perhaps, really, this fat man is tender-hearted?' As if to give the lie to my thoughts, at that very instant I heard him laugh, clink glasses and fix a rendezvous, and I began to have hopes of him, and his science, once more.

And now the office was emptying, it was getting late and people were slowly drifting away. To avoid having to say goodbye to the last stragglers, I began making an inventory of the works of art Max had received as a token of gratitude and friendship at each new stage of his glorious career. There were tables full of them, at least fifteen hundred *objets d'art* in cast metals and, curiously enough, most of them were monumental inkstands. Inkstands in bronze or brass, inkstands in gold or silver, inkstands in shagreen, inkstands in Morocco leather; inkstands in the form of Buddha, lions, horseshoes, lucky charms, railway engines, tenders and mail vans; inkstands in the shape of towers, bridges, boilers, railway stations, signals and water-towers; inkstands composed of groups of naked women, elaborate weapons, shells, crystals, gold nuggets, nuts and bolts; inkstands surmounted by busts or figurines of State leaders, or ornamented with the insignia of corporations and companies, the coats of arms of various communes, mottoes, palms, crowns, figures of Victory, cogwheels, anvils, pliers and hammers.

I was just deciphering the commemorative inscriptions with which, like the pedestals, these inkstands of honour were overburdened on all four sides – the dock-workers of Santa Fé, the staff at the Bécon-les-Bruyères railway station, the municipal council of Winnipeg, the French-Canadians, the Spanish, the English, the Germans and the Brazilians had all been determined to have their signatures engraved, and I was astounded at the number of dedications in Russian, Greek, Turkish, Arabic, Chinese and Copt, which I could not understand, when Max laid his big paw on my shoulder.

I thought I would faint with shock. It was time. I had to speak to him.

'Would you like me to bring you my collection of decorations, titles and diplomas as well? Now then, you old joker, what tricks have you got up your sleeve, and how goes it with the cinema?'

'Oh! . . . Max . . . I wound all that up ages ago . . . I . . .'

'Ah! That's why they don't write about you in the newspapers any more! But didn't I tell you so, right from the start?' he cried triumphantly. 'Believe me, Hollywood is the only place for a star who . . .'

'But Max, I . . .'

'Come along, you'll come back to the house and have dinner with me, won't you?'

'Impossible, Max, no, I . . . I am leaving again immediately . . . my car's outside, I . . . I . . .'

'Not the same one you had on Armistice night, eh?' And Max gave a great shout of laughter.

'But what's the matter with you?' he asked suddenly, 'I can't recognize you any more. . . . Confound it, I'm going completely blind,' he growled, dragging me under the chandelier.

Then, leaning over me and peering closely at me with his dead eyes: 'My God, how you've changed! What is it?'

'Max . . . I wanted. . . .' How could I tell him? . . . 'I beg your pardon, Max . . . I wanted, I wanted. . . . How is Mme Hyène?'

'Jesus Christ, man, are you mad?' Max cried, squeezing my wrists. 'That's the first time a friend has ever asked after Mme Hyène's health! Thank you, anyway,' he added after wiping his glasses. 'Thank you, she is very well. But you, what's the matter with you - tell me, are you ill?'

'No . . . but . . . I . . . the scales . . . Mme Hyène . . .'

'That's enough! Stop fooling now. Sit down here and let's talk seriously. I'm listening. It's bad, is it? Mireille . . .'

'Exactly, Max, my little girl is dying!'

And I told him everything, my anguish, the whole drama, how I had met her, why I had come, what I was hoping for from him. I wept scalding hot tears, shamelessly, and for the first time in my life.

Max listened to me without budging.

I went on talking and talking, for when one is recounting one's miseries one never comes to the end of it. I got into deep water by alluding yet again to the scales that had motivated my visit, and then made matters worse by apologizing for my indiscretion.

It was becoming painful, so Max interrupted me to declare: 'You are absolutely wrong there, my poor friend, these two cases have absolutely nothing in common. Mme Max Hyène is not an intellectual, she is nothing more than a constipated woman. Nor does she present any of those mental symptoms you tell me you have constantly observed in Mireille. The only point I can concede here is that Mme Max Hyène, at the most, suffers from hysteria, but then her hysteria is disguised and strictly localized and, at the moment, they're giving her purges of mercury. Certainly - how can I put it? - this non-activity, this passivity, this laziness of the bodily functions is accompanied by a great laziness of the mind, so much so that I really couldn't tell you which is the dominant factor, but the moral torpor, the infantile habits, the childish reasoning and the trivial occupations . . . all that is quite normal in a shallow woman who has neither temperament nor curiosity, and whose only scruples of conscience are of an exclusively hygienic order. Nowadays it is quite understandable that medicine has become the religion of women who have no other faith, and it is equally understandable that I should feel no undue alarm at my wife's . . . I was going to say vice, but let's say illness, or, better still, mania, mild mania, given that Mme Max Hyène has always had a petty nature, a weak head, a narrow outlook and a colourless personality, the absolute antipodes of your unfortunate little girl, who must be a passionate creature? . . . No? . . . Well, then, I don't understand any more. . . .

'What I don't understand in the case of Mireille, who is so sweet and so communicative,' Max went on after a moment's reflection, 'is this repudiation of the natural functions of life, this horror which afflicts her, this disgust, this restraining of all her sensibilities, this repression which leads her to rebel against herself, this frenzy which makes her want to do herself an injury. What have they been able to do for her? You don't know what has happened to her? She is no longer in control of herself, and yet I have a distinct impression that she is denying herself. If I have understood you correctly, her physical problems are due to her moral sufferings. In direct contrast to Mme Max Hyène, her torment is essentially of a mental order . . .

'She's an imaginative girl. You tell me she doesn't want to, that she says "no", but you haven't told me what she's saying "no" to, and what it is she doesn't want to do? I wonder what she is recoiling from, as if she was afraid of falling, and, if she is holding *back*, what is she holding *on* to? You don't know? . . . No? . . . Come along, my poor friend, I am going to make you confess. Tell me, why is it that throughout this entire recital you have just given me, you called her *my little girl* and never once 'my wife', or simply 'Mireille?'

'. . . ?'

'Yes, I understand, but is that one of those little nicknames lovers like to call each other, or is it a habitual way of thinking?'

'Oh, Max, we were like brother and sister!'

'What, precisely, do you mean by that?'

'But Max . . .'

'Answer me! Is that just a manner of speaking, or is it your habitual way of being together?'

'. . . ?'

'Yes, I know what I'm talking about. Now, answer me frankly, what was she like when you made love - a volcano?'

'But Max . . .'

'Frigid, then?'

'Oh no, Max.'

'Answer me!'

'She didn't want to.'

'Never?'

'No.'

'Why?'

'She was afraid.'

'Just as I thought. But what was she afraid of?'

'I don't know.'

'And you lived together?'

'For seven years.'

'And you've never cheated on her?'

'Never.'

'And you've never taken her?'

'Never.'

'And she has never given herself?'

'Never.'

'You should have raped her. But what were you thinking of, my friend?'

'I don't know . . . she was such a beautiful little girl!'

'And you loved her?'

'Yes.'

'And you were happy?'

'Oh yes!'

Max Hyène meditated. He was turning a compass round and round in his fingers. He had forgotten me.

'. . . Love . . . there are women who have hysterical pregnancies, why shouldn't a cerebral type . . . a case of spontaneous combustion . . . that's how monsters are born. . . .'

What conclusion would he come to?

It was past midnight. My car was waiting for me. I fled in consternation.

. . . .

Cylinder Nine

. . . .

Saint-Gervais, 13th June 1925

What am I going to do in Paris?

No more booze, no more women, no, no more alcohol.

This telegram arrives for me:

DAN YACK MONTJOLY SAINT-GERVAIS HAUTE-SAVOIE SENDING YOU
TRACTA TODAY BY ROAD STOP ALWAYS AT YOUR ORDERS STOP
ESSOR.

What in the world is a *Tracta*, and what am I going to do with it?
At last I shall leave.

And Pierre has come back, empty-handed of course, from Saint-
Nicolas-de-Véroce; Lucienne won't hear of going to Paris with
me. As I expected. Well, so much the better.

Ah! So much the better, so much the better, so much the better!
I shall remain chaste. But what am I going to do in Paris?

Pierre kept jabbering at me, so I turned him out.

'What a bitch that silly tart is!' he said. 'If I were you, I'd give
her a clout round the chops to teach her a lesson. All the same,
she's a nice bit of skirt, eh?'

'Oh shut up, Pierre! Look, here's a cheque. Tomorrow I'm going
back to Paris. You've only got to fill it in, then you can have your
money. You can take everything I've left at the chalet, too - my
gun, my boots, the whole bloody lot.'

And I handed him a blank cheque.

'What's this?' he asked me, turning it over and over. 'I can't read. . . .'

I explained that all he had to do was present it at the English bank opposite the Majestic and they would give him cash for it.

'Jesus Christ! We'll have a drink on that!' he cried. 'But what's written on it?'

'As much as you like, Pierre, how much do you need?'

'Put down twenty francs, boss, that'll do me.'

I wrote out a cheque for two hundred thousand francs in his name and gave it to Pierre.

'Aren't you coming?'

'No, Pierre, goodbye.'

And Pierre went out without knowing what he had in his hand.

Will this money make him happy? Well, I wish him the best of luck.

As for me, my life is over, I feel sure of it.

. . . .

I was in the café on the corner, playing skittles, when the nurse from the sanatorium came to tell me that Mireille was dead.

'At what time?' I asked him.

'On the stroke of midday,' said this man.

He was a big fat fellow.

Why did I ask him about the time? An idiotic question.

The man was all out of breath from running and seemed upset, or perhaps he was pretending to be upset. In any case he bent down to talk to me and observe me from below, to see how I would react to the news, and I didn't like that. I ordered him a drink so as to cut short his condolences.

'White?'

'Red.'

'Right, then, a litre of red, Mademoiselle, and three glasses.'

The third glass was for Pierre, my partner at skittles.

That litre of red!

The skittle-alley was scented by an acacia which shed its white flowers into our glasses. There was a gentle breeze. The skittles flew right and left. Next to us some railway workers were playing, but soon they would be obliged to go and meet the train we could already hear grinding down in the bottom of the valley. They were playing violently, determined to score points.

There was a litre of red on the table and three men, three men sitting round the table, three men who were not saying a word. The glasses were filled, they emptied them. The acacia shook down its petals.

The railwaymen went off at the double, pushing and shoving one another.

I remember, too, a wasp that came and settled on my cheek.

As happens when you have a car accident, all these minute details imprinted themselves on my mind in a fraction of a second.

It is still very vivid to me.

Perfect recall.

But I also remember my stupefaction when I realized that the wine was good.

So, life was still possible, one did not drop dead on the spot? That litre of red!

If I'd had my way, I should have gone on drinking. I wanted to order a second, a third, a fourth, but the man, the fat man whom I suddenly began to detest, that damned nurse who had just rinsed the wine round in his glass before swallowing the last drop, stood up and said: 'Excuse me, Monsieur, but I'm off duty now. My good lady's waiting for me, it's time to go home for lunch.'

And he said goodbye, shaking me warmly by the hand.

That fat man gave me the creeps.

So, was he the last person to see Mireille alive? I followed him with my eyes. He crossed the little square without hurrying, his backside wobbling, his flat feet turned out, his nurse's overalls rolled up under his arm, as he carried all my thoughts away with him. He was going home to his soup.

As the man stopped two or three times, scratching his head and looking back at us with yearning spaniel eyes, I sent Pierre after him, as soon as he'd turned the corner, to give him a tip.

So, it was all over.

I, too, left in my turn.

And it seems that, after all, one does not go mad, since I suddenly found myself on my balcony, this same balcony where I am sitting now, and it was a fine, serene evening, like this one. But then I inspected the sky. I had been to fetch my field-glasses. I looked for the eagles, as I wanted to go and kill them next day. Today I look inward, into myself. There is nothing there. Nothing left. I am finished.

. . . .

I had told Pierre to prepare the ropes and the crampons. I wanted to reach the Aiguille de Varens before dawn, follow the crest of the rocky wall that overhangs the Platé desert between Le Coloney and La Pelouse, so as to reach a point above the eagles' eyrie I had sighted, and then let myself down on the end of a rope to surprise the birds in the nest.

This expedition proved to be one of the greatest disappointments in my life. When I reached the eyrie, the birds had flown. The nest had been plundered. Someone must have been there before me. There wasn't even an egg left. Nothing but bird droppings, nothing but shit.

. . . .

What am I going to do in Paris?

The *Tracta* has arrived. She's very low-slung, exceptionally light, has a front-wheel drive and can reach speeds of 180 k.p.h.

She is powerful and easy to handle, her terrific pull and the eager way she cleaves the air makes you feel you are flying. Once you've experienced it, you will never forget that sensation. And the way she takes corners is a dream! 'It's not a car, it's a plane, the aeroplane of the road,' said the mechanic who drove her from Paris for me.

Good. So much the better.

I give this boy the train fare back to Paris, he can take the de-luxe train if he likes. And I settle myself at the wheel, alone.

He looks so unhappy, so annoyed at being left behind, that I give him my most charming smile.

My last smile.

I grip the steering-wheel, press the starter, put her in gear, let the clutch in and roar off.

I am going to chance my luck once again.

If only I could crash into something and smash my face in!

. . . .

101 rue du Parc-Montsouris, 1st September 1925

Here I am.

I'm in Paris.

I didn't know you could live so simply in Paris.

I have returned to Paris and this is how I have organized my life: I have bought a whole floor, the sixth, in a large modern building, number 101, in the rue du Parc-Montsouris. I have had the partition walls knocked down because I like large, empty rooms.

Oh, and I'm camping! The only modern comfort I have retained is the bathroom. Otherwise I'm just camping. As I did in the bush. I have slung my hammock in front of the fireplace in the drawing-room and all the rooms which look out at the back, over the courtyard, are full of logs, fine round logs that I saw into two or three lengths. I do my cooking as if I were in the open air, on a wood fire. My bathroom is really magnificent, with a complicated system of showers and a little pool for my tortoise. I have bought myself a large tortoise from the quai de la Mégisserie.

I have also bought a stunning electrolier, some film studio lights, some surgical lamps, a strip of neon lighting and a mercury vapour apparatus which inscribes my name on the ceiling. When I want to sleep, I hang an arc lamp over my head. When it's night outside, it's daytime in my place. I hypnotize myself. Sometimes I sleep, sometimes I dream, sometimes I feel dizzy, then I swing in my hammock as if I were on the high seas; if it weren't for the neighbours, I would install a whole range of sirens, or, as in the basements in Saint-Didier, a sample display equipped with every type of electric horn, and I would amuse myself by sounding them at night. But at night it is quiet in my place, because most of the time I am not there.

I go out.

I walk around.

I spend my time in the streets.

Very often I go to work at Les Halles, where I have found a job with a florist, or I unload crates of eggs or stems of bananas.

I don't drink any more, but I still smoke a lot.

I smoke all day long on my balcony.

I have a balcony that runs right along the whole façade. In the mornings I smoke serenely in a corner, then I shift imperceptibly to the left, keeping pace with the movement of the sun.

I really enjoy smoking up there. I feel serene. My street is very quiet, with the same cars passing every day at the same time, a little flurry of activity at midday, and the parade of nannies with their little perambulators taking their charges to the park in the afternoons. The sky is immense above the dense foliage. I hear the whistle of a rare train on the Ceinture line, the bugle of the station-master on the Sceaux line, the quacking of water-fowl on the lake. I tried listening to the radio, but I soon got rid of it, and now I am going to get rid of my dictaphone too. That machine annoys me. I have nothing more to say to it.

Today is my birthday.

I am fifty-two years old.

I have been to see my son.

This morning, coming back from Les Halles, I took him a little pink rabbit.

For a long time I had been roaming round the huts on the boulevard Jourdan, and I had taken all the necessary steps to adopt him. In the orphanage there were plenty of little Russian orphans. I chose an eleven-year-old boy, pale, sad, with eyes like Hedwiga's. His name is Nicolas.

I shall call him Dan Yack, like me.

I shall teach him to laugh.

I shall make him laugh.

And, for a start, the three of us are crawling about on all fours on the parquet floor, me, my son, and the little pink rabbit, in my big empty apartment. . . .

.   .   .   .

Paris, 1917
Santos, 1927
L'Escarayol - La Redonne, 1927
Santos, 1928
Rue des Marroniers, 1928
Les Artigaux - Le Bastat, 1928
Le Tremblay-sur-Mauldre, 1929
Recorded on the dictaphone somewhere in the country: summer 1929.

Peter Owen Modern Classics

If you have enjoyed this book you may like to try some of the other Peter Owen paperback reprints listed below. **The Peter Owen Modern Classics** series was launched in 1998 to bring some of our internationally acclaimed authors and their works, first published by Peter Owen in hardback, to a contemporary readership.

To order books or a free catalogue or for further information on these or any other Peter Owen titles, please contact the **Sales Department, Peter Owen Ltd, 73 Kenway Road, London SW5 0RE, UK** tel: **++ 44 (0)20 7373 5628 or ++ 44 (0)20 7370 6093**, fax: **++ 44 (0)20 7373 6760**, e-mail: **sales@peterowen.com** or visit our website at **www.peterowen.com**

Guillaume Apollinaire
LES ONZE MILLE VERGES

In 1907 Guillaume Apollinaire, one of the most original and influential poets of the twentieth century, turned his hand to the novel. He produced two books for the clandestine erotica market, the finer of these being *Les Onze Mille Verges*. One of the most masterful and hilarious novels of all time, it was pronounced owlishly by Picasso to be Apollinaire's masterpiece.

'A vigorous and highly readable translation.' – *Times Literary Supplement*

0 7206 1100 8   £9.95

Paul Bowles
MIDNIGHT MASS

Chosen by the author from his best, these superlative short stories reveal Paul Bowles at his peak. They offer insights into the mysteries of *kif* and the majesty of the desert, the meeting of alien cultures and the clash between modern and ancient, Islam and Christianity, logic and superstition. Set in Morocco, Thailand and Sri Lanka, these stories reverberate with vision and, like Bowles's novels, they are universal in their appeal.

'His short stories are among the best ever written by an American.' – Gore Vidal

0 7206 1083 4   £9.95

POINTS IN TIME

Here Bowles focuses on Morocco, his home for many decades, condensing experience, emotion and the whole history of a people into a series of short, brilliant pieces. He takes the reader on a journey through the Moroccan centuries, pausing at points along the way to create resonant images of the country and the beliefs and characteristics of its inhabitants.

'His plain and compact prose makes this a wholly

satisfying book.' – *Literary Review*

'Persuasive prose which leaves one with a very strong and distinct flavour of landscape and people.' – *Gay Times*

0 7206 1137 7   £8.50

THEIR HEADS ARE GREEN

First published in 1963, this is an account of Bowles's experiences in Morocco and his journeys to the Sahara, which influenced the classic *The Sheltering Sky*, as well as his travels through Mexico, Turkey and Sri Lanka. With his exceptional gift for penetrating beyond the picturesque or exotic aspects of the countries he describes, he evokes the unique characteristics of both people and places.

'Few writers have Bowles's skill in evocation while making the familiar something new and extraordinary.' – *The Times*

0 7206 1077 X   £9.95

UP ABOVE THE WORLD

Dr Slade and his wife are on holiday in Latin America when they meet Grove, a young man of striking good looks and charm and his beautiful seventeen-year-old mistress. An apparently chance encounter, it opens the door to a nightmare as the Slades find themselves being sucked in by lives whose relevance to their own they cannot understand. Oiled by a cocktail of drugs and dark relationships, the Slades are lured on another journey: a terrifying trip where the only guides are fantasy, hallucination and death.

Brilliantly written, with the poetic control that has always characterized Bowles's work, *Up Above the World* is a masterpiece of cold, relentless terror.

'Sex, drugs, fantasies and the machinery of derangement . . . Bowles's overpowering void descends on the mind and heart like a hypnotic spell.' — *New York Times Book Review*

0 7206 1087 7   £9.95

Blaise Cendrars
TO THE END OF THE WORLD

The narrative of this novel shifts between a Foreign Legion barracks in North Africa and the theatres, cafés, dosshouses and police headquarters of post-war Paris. The central character in this *roman-à-clef* is a septuagenarian actress whose affair with a young deserter from the Foreign Legion is jeopardized by the murder of a barman. *To the End of the World* is not pure invention. Like all Cendrars's works it has some basis in his nomadic life; but this original and often very funny portrayal of the Paris of the late 1940s is obviously the product of an abundant imagination.

'There is nothing like reading Cendrars.' — *Independent*

0 7206 1097 4   £9.95

DAN YACK

Dan Yack is an eccentric English millionaire ship owner, a notorious hell-raiser, and the envy of all St Petersburg. He is also the alter ego of his creator, Blaise Cendrars. This strange travel yarn begins with Dan Yack finding out that he is no longer wanted by his lover, Hedwiga. Regaining consciousness after a mammoth drinking bout, he impulsively invites three artists to accompany him on a world voyage via the Antarctic. After a hard winter the sun finally returns, but no one could predict the surreal disaster that is about to unfold, a scenario involving a plum pudding, whales, women and World War I.

'A kind of jazz-age super-cocktail, a swirling cauldron of the outrageous, the orgiastic and the surreal.' – *Guardian*

'Mad, vicious, amusing and beautiful.' – *Time Out*

'A virtuoso performance.' – *Observer*

'Tintin for grown-ups.' – *Irish Times*

0 7206 1157 1   £9.95

THE CONFESSIONS OF DAN YACK

This continues the adventures of Dan Yack. He tells the story of his love for Mireille whom he meets in a crowded tabac in a Paris gone mad on Armistice Night, 1918. This love transforms Dan Yack's life: he abandons his women, gives up his fast cars and debauchery to marry this convent-educated girl of his dreams. To indulge her fantasies he launches her as a film star and casts her in wraith-like roles inspired by Edgar Allen Poe. But before long Mireille is struck by a mysterious and fatal illness, the psychological origins of which raise disturbing questions about the nature of their relationship. Whereas Dan Yack's previous memoir celebrated his exploits with malicious

bravado, this is a bittersweet memoir of love and loss, shot through with profound melancholy and a palpable sense of psycho-sexual disturbance.

'A beautifully written work, memorable and compelling and superbly translated. It makes one reach out for everything else he ever wrote.' – *Sunday Telegraph*

'Discovery of the year, a box-fresh piece of 1920s Parisiana.' – Books of the Year, *Independent,*

0 7206 1158 X   £9.95

Jean Cocteau
LE LIVRE BLANC

This 'white paper' on homosexual love was first published anonymously in France by Cocteau's contemporary Maurice Sachs and was at once decried as obscene. The semi-autobiographical narrative describes a youth's love affairs with a succession of boys and men during the early years of this century. The young man's self-deceptive attempts to find fulfilment, first through women and then by way of the Church, are movingly conveyed, and the book ends with a plea for homosexuality to be accepted without censure. The book includes woodcuts by the author.

'A wonderful book.' — *Gay Times*

0 7206 1081 8   £8.50

Colette
DUO and LE TOUTOUNIER

These two linked novels are works of Colette's maturity. In *Duo* Colette observes, with astuteness and perception, two characters whose marriage is foundering on the wife's infidelity. Acting out the crisis, Alice and Michel have the stage to themselves so that nothing is allowed to distract from the marital dialogue. *Le Toutounier* continues Alice's story after Michel's death and her move to Paris. There she and her two sisters live in a shabby, homely apartment; fiercely independent, reticent, hard-working, needing men but showing little sign of loving them, they speak a private language and seek comfort in the indestructible sofa (*toutounier*) of their childhood.

'Drenched with her talent at its best.' — *Sunday Times*

0 7206 1069 9   £9.95

Lawrence Durrell
POPE JOAN

In this superb adaptation of a novel by the nineteenth-century Greek author Emmanuel Royidis, Lawrence Durrell traces the remarkable history of a young woman who travelled across Europe in the ninth century disguised as a monk, acquired great learning and ruled over Christendom for two years as Pope John VIII before her death in childbirth. When *Papissa Joanna* was first published in Athens in 1886 it created a sensation. The book was banned and its author excommunicated. It nevertheless brought him fame and the work established itself in the history of modern Greek literature. Subsequently Durrell created a masterpiece in its own right, a dazzling concoction presented with the deftest touch.

'A sharp satire . . . acutely funny . . . salacious.' – *Spectator*

'The most remarkable of Durrell's adaptations was his brilliant version of Emmanuel Royidis's novel.' – *The Times*

'One of the funniest novels ever written . . . A true classic.' – *Punch*

0 7206 1065 6   £9.95

Shusaku Endo
WONDERFUL FOOL

Gaston Bonaparte, a young Frenchman, visits Tokyo to stay with his pen-friend Takamori. His appearance is a bitter disappointment to his new friends and his behaviour causes them acute embarrassment. He is a trusting person with a simple love for others and continues to trust them even after they have demonstrated deceit and betrayal. He spends his time making friends with street children, stray dogs, prostitutes and gangsters. Endo charts his misadventures with sharp irony, satire and objectivity.

'The perfect guide in the form of fiction to Tokyo and the Japanese experience.' — Grahame Greene

0 7206 1080 X   £9.95

Jean Giono
TWO RIDERS ON THE STORM

Set in the remote hills of Provence, where the lives of the inhabitants are moulded along fiercely passionate lines, this is the story of two brothers, members of a family renowned for its brutality and bound together with ties stronger than those of ordinary filial love. Yet this affection turns to hatred after the elder brother kills a wild horse with a single blow at a country fair and becomes the local wrestling champion. As his strength increases and his fame spreads, the younger sibling's jealousy causes this bond to snap. The end, when it comes, is a violent – and deadly – confrontation.

'Giono gives us a world he lives in, a world of dream, passion and reality.' – Henry Miller

'It has a timeless fairytale quality . . . zestful and humorous.' – *Sunday Times*

'Violent but beautiful . . . a novelist of great originality.' – *Spectator*

0 7206 1159 8   £9.95

Hermann Hesse
DEMIAN

Published shortly after the First World War, *Demian* is one of Hermann Hesse's finest novels. Emil Sinclair boasts of a theft that he has not committed and finds himself blackmailed by a bully. He turns to Max Demian, in whom he finds a friend and spiritual mentor. This strangely self-possessed figure is able to lure him out of his ordinary home life and convince him of an existing alternative world of corruption and evil. In progressing from an orthodox education through to philosophical mysticism, Emil's search for self-awareness culminates in a meeting with Demian's mother – symbol and personification of motherhood.

'One of the most elevated spiritual and ethical allegories I have ever read . . . extremely readable.' – *Listener*

'A moving fable of spiritual growth.' – *Observer*

0 7206 1130 X   £9.95

GERTRUDE

Gertrude portrays the life and emotional development of a young composer, Kuhn, who finds success in his art under the sway of Heinrich Muoth, a melancholy and self-destructive opera singer, and the gentle self-assured Gertrude. Kuhn falls in love with Gertrude but she falls for Muoth, and their unhappy marriage becomes a metaphor for the opposing forces of the Dionysian and the Apollonian.

'It would be a pity to miss this book – it has such a rare flavour of truth and simplicity.' – Stevie Smith, *Observer*

'There is a freshness and authenticity about these characters.' – *Times Literary Supplement*

0 7206 1169 5   £9.95

JOURNEY TO THE EAST

The narrator of this allegorical tale travels through time and space in a search of ultimate truth. This pilgrimage to the East covers both real and imagined lands and takes place not only in the last century but also in the Middle Ages and the Renaissance. The fellow travellers, too, are both real and fictitious and include Plato, Pythagorus, Don Quixote, Tristram Shandy and Baudelaire. Like the better-known *Siddartha*, this is a timeless novel of broad appeal, with an easy lyricism and a well-composed symmetry of style.

0 7206 1131 8   £8.50

NARCISSUS AND GOLDMUND

Narcissus is a teacher at a medieval monastery, and Goldmund his favourite pupil. The latter runs away in pursuit of love, living a wanderer's life which brings him both pain and ecstasy. Narcissus remains behind, detached from the world in prayer and meditation. Their eventual reunion brings into focus the diversity between artist and thinker, Dionysian and Apollonian. Thought by some to be Hesse's greatest novel, this is a classic of contemporary literature.

'Deeply moving and richly poetic, this brilliant fusion of concepts is astonishing in its simplicity and power.'
— *Birmingham Post*

0 7206 1102 4   £12.50

PETER CAMENZIND

In this semi-autobiographical novel, Peter Camenzind is an introverted Swiss peasant boy who becomes a student at Zurich University where he seems destined for some academic post. Yet he does not choose this path: perturbed by what he perceives to be the thankless and turbulent unrest of human nature, he seeks his salvation through self-knowledge in the manner of a Romantic hero. But salvation in casual love affairs and in the bars and literary salons of European cities proves elusive. Finally he turns to St Francis of Assisi, but personal sublimation after the example of the saint still does not give his mind rest. It is not until he returns to his own village to care for his dying father that he can find the path that leads back to himself.

'Explores in frequently moving terms the early manhood of a genius.' – *Daily Telegraph*

'Liberating, fiercely undated, inimitable. Hesse should be read in chunks.' – *Guardian*

'A masterpiece' – *London Evening Standard*

0 7206 1168 7   £9.95

Anna Kavan
ASYLUM PIECE

First published sixty years ago, *Asylum Piece* today ranks as one of the most extraordinary and terrifying evocations of human madness ever written. This collection of stories, mostly interlinked and largely autobiographical, chart the descent of the narrator from the onset of neurosis to final incarceration at a Swiss clinic. The sense of paranoia, of persecution by a foe or force that is never given a name evokes Kafka, though Kavan's deeply personal, restrained and almost foreign-accented style has no true model. The same characters who recur throughout – the protagonist's unhelpful 'adviser', the friend/lover who abandons her at the clinic and an assortment of deluded companions – are sketched without a trace of rage, self-pity or sentiment.

0 7206 1123 7   £9.95

THE PARSON

The Parson of the title is not a cleric but an upright young army officer so named for his apparent prudishness. On leave, he meets Rejane, a rich and beguiling beauty, the woman of his dreams. The days that he spends with Rejane, riding in and exploring the wild moorland, have their enchantment, but she grows restless in this desolate landscape. Though doubtless in love with him, she discourages any intimacy, until she persuades him to take her to a sinister castle situated on a treacherous headland . . . *The Parson* is less a tale of unrequited love than exploration of divided selves, momentarily locked in an unequal embrace. Passion is revealed as a play of the senses as well as a destructive force. Comparisons have been made between this writer and Poe, Kafka and Thomas Hardy, but the presence of her trademark themes, juxtaposed and set in her risk-taking prose, mark *The Parson* as one-hundred-per-cent Kavan.

0 7206 1140 7   £8.95

SLEEP HAS HIS HOUSE

A daring synthesis of memoir and surrealist experimentation, *Sleep Has His House* charts the stages of the subject's withdrawal from contact with the daylight world of received reality. Flashes of experience from childhood, adolescence and youth are described in what Kavan terms 'night-time language' – a heightened prose that frees these events from their gloomy associations. The novel suggests that we have all spoken this dialect in childhood and in our dreams, but these thoughts can only be decoded by contemplation in the dark.

Kavan maintained that the plot of a book is only point of departure, beyond which she tries to reveal that side of life which is never seen by the waking eye but which dreams and drugs can illuminate. She spent the last ten years of her life literally and metaphorically shutting out the light; the startling discovery of *Sleep Has His House* is how much these night-time illuminations reveal her joy for the living world. The novel startled with its strangeness in 1948. Today it is one of Kavan's most acclaimed books.

'Possibly one of her most interesting books, a near masterpiece in the imaginative speculations of those whose paradise simultaneously contains their hell.' – *The Times*

'Anna Kavan's "night-time language" is in no way obscure: on the contrary, her dreams are as carefully notated as paintings by Dalí or de Chirico.' – *New Statesman*

'Her writing is magnificent. It is a fascinating clinical casebook of her obsessions and the effects of drugs on her imagination . . . in the tradition of the great writers on drug literature, de Quincey, Wilkie Collins, Coleridge.' – *Daily Telegraph*

'A testament of remarkable, if feverish beauty.' – *Guardian*

0 7206 1129 6   £9.95

WHO ARE YOU?

Who Are You? is a sparse depiction of the hopeless, emotional polarity of a young couple and their doomed marriage spent in a remote, tropical hell. She – described only as 'the girl' – is young, sophisticated and sensitive; he, 'Mr Dog-Head', is a thug and heavy drinker who rapes her, otherwise passing his time bludgeoning rats with a tennis racket. Together with a visiting stranger, 'Suede Boots', who urges the woman to escape until he is banished by her husband, these characters live through the same situations twice. Their identities are equally real – or unreal – in each case. With slight variation in the background and the novel's atmosphere, neither the outcome nor the characters themselves are quite the same the second time. The constant question of the jungle 'brain-fever' bird remains unanswered – 'Who are you?' First published in 1963, *Who Are You?* was reissued to widespread acclaim in 1973.

'To write about this finely economical book in any terms other than its own is cruelly to distort the near-perfection of the original text. There is a vision here which dismays.' – Robert Nye, *Guardian*

'*Who Are You?* is accomplished and complete . . . so fully imagined, so finely described in spare, effective prose, that it is easy to suspend disbelief.' – Nina Bawden, *Daily Telegraph*

'Lots of fun to read, sprouts with a macabre imagination and is, no question, a classic.' – *Sunday Telegraph*

0 7206 1150 4   £8.95

Yukio Mishima
CONFESSIONS OF A MASK

This autobiographical novel, regarded as Mishima's finest book, is the haunting story of a Japanese boy's homosexual awakening during and after the Second World War. Detailing his progress from an isolated childhood through adolescence to manhood, including an abortive love affair with a classmate's sister, it reveals the inner life of a boy's preoccupation with death. The books continuing appeal attests to the novel's enduring themes of fantasy, despair and alienation.

'A terrific and astringent beauty . . . a work of art.' — *Times Literary Supplement*

0 7206 1031 1   £11.95

Anaïs Nin
CHILDREN OF THE ALBATROSS

Children of the Albatross is conceived as a series of lyrical descriptions of the experience of Djuna, a former ballet dancer, and her circle. The central account of the novel is her love affair with a seventeen-year-old youth who finally leaves her. On the surface a portrayal of the clash between autumnal and adolescent passions, this is an insightful tale about an older woman who, as the result of an unhappy childhood, rebels against male tyranny and instinctively looks for the child – one in whom 'the arteries of faith have not hardened' – rather than the man in her lovers.

'A novel that oscillates with sensibility like a cat's whisker.' – *Sunday Telegraph*

'A finely spun web of feeling and insight into the feminine condition . . . Exquisitely written.' – *Scotsman*

0 7206 1165 5

THE FOUR-CHAMBERED HEART

This continues the adventures of Djuna, the eccentric star of *Children of the Albatross*. Djuna is in love with a husky and feckless Guatemalan guitar player. They make their home on a squalid, leaky houseboat anchored on the Seine which, like their relationship, is destined to go nowhere. His volatile personality and bohemian outlook ensures that the dream of accomplishing the very something that Djuna awakes in him will never come to anything. For her part, the self-sacrificing Djuna is forced to accommodate into her home his sickly wife, to whom he is tied by a half-blind complicity in her desire to exploit all who come within range.

'Her prose is like a shaft of sunlight, a cold clear colour that can be broken up suddenly into many prismatic hues. Of her books, *The Four-Chambered* Heart is undoubtedly the most successful . . . the book expresses the destruction of poetic imagination by the hard facts of life; but the expression is done in the manner of poetry.' – *Irish Times*

0 7206 1155 5   £9.95

COLLAGES

Collages explores a world of fantasy and dreams through an eccentric young painter. A radical work when published in the early 1960s, in it Nin dispensed with normal structural convention and allowed her characters to wander freely in space and time in an attempt to describe life with the disconnected clarity of a dream in which hip and freakish lives intersect or merge. Making a rapid escape from her sick father in Vienna, Renate begins her sensation-seeking travel odyssey accompanied by a gay Norwegian man who allows her to open one of his Chinese boxes and read a chapter of his past each time she finds his absence unbearable. *Collages* is a shifting notebook indelibly inscribed with Nin's humour, invention and unrivalled gift for sensuous description.

'Perfectly told fables, and prose which is so daringly elaborate, so accurately timed that it is not entirely surprising to hear her compared to Proust.' – *Times Literary Supplement*

'Nin's writing is spare, and sharply perceptive, her imaginative vision quite remarkable.' – *Scotsman*

'A delight.' – *Independent*

0 7206 1145 8   £9.95

LADDERS TO FIRE

This poetic, sensual novel, the first in the 'Cities of the Interior' series, focuses on the lives of a group of women as they undergo a period of emotional and sexual development. They record their experiences as they struggle to understand both themselves and each other. As with most of Nin's novels, *Ladders to Fire* draws its inspiration from her confessional diaries begun in 1914 at the age of eleven. It dates from the period when Anaïs Nin moved to New York, a time also explored in the film *Henry and June*.

'It is refreshing to find a 1940s' novel so firmly situated in the realms of female consciousness and so rooted in a conviction of the validity of female desire.' – *Scotsman*

'Nin writes sensitively, with psychological training as well as insight . . . she has a subcutaneous interest in her characters and Lawrence's sixth sense.' – *Times Literary Supplement*

0 7206 1162 8   £9.95

Boris Pasternak
THE LAST SUMMER

By the author of *Dr Zhivago*, and his only other completed work of fiction, *The Last Summer* is set in Russia during the winter of 1916, when Serezha visits his married sister. Tired after a long journey, he falls into a restless sleep and half remembers, half dreams the incidents of the last summer of peace before the First World War. As tutor in a wealthy, unsettled Moscow household, he focuses his intense romanticism on Mrs Arild, the employer's paid companion, while spending his nights with the prostitute Sashka and others. In this evocation of the past, the characters are subtly etched against their social backgrounds, and Pasternak imbues the commonplace with his own intense and poetic vision.

'A concerto in prose.' — V.S. Pritchett

0 7206 1099 0   £8.50

Cesare Pavese
THE DEVIL IN THE HILLS

The Devil in the Hills is the most personal of Pavese's novels, an elegiac celebration of lost youth set in the landscape of his own boyhood: the hills, vineyards and villages of Piedmont. Three young men while away the summer talking, drinking – rarely sleeping – and there is an overwhelming sense that it is the last summer that they will be able to indulge such pleasures. In contrast to their feelings of transcience, the leisure of their new, wealthy acquaintance, Poli, fascinates them. For a while they linger in his world, in his decaying villa, half appalled by his cocaine addiction, his blasphemy, his corrupt circle of friends, but none the less mesmerized until autumn creeps upon the hillside and the moment of leave-taking arrives . . .

'In this remarkable author, the compassionate moralist and the instinctive poet go hand in hand.' – *Scotsman*

'The Devil in the Hills shows how ahead of his time Pavese was.' – *The Times*

'Erotic, but extraordinarily delicate and controlled.' – *Guardian*

0 7206 1118 0   £9.95

THE MOON AND THE BONFIRE

Anguilla is a successful businessman lured home from California to the Piedmontese village where he was fostered by peasants. But after twenty years much has changed. Slowly, he is able to piece together the past and relates it to what he finds in the present. He looks at the lives and sometimes violent fates of the villagers he has known from childhood, setting the poverty, ignorance or indifference that binds them to these hills and valleys against the beauty of the landscape and the rhythm of the seasons. With stark realism and muted compassion Pavese weaves the strands together and brings them to a stark and poignant climax.

'Wonderfully written, beautifully translated.' – *Sunday Times*

'Reminds us again how good a writer Pavese was.' – *Sunday Telegraph*

0 7206 1119 9   £9.95

Mervyn Peake
A BOOK OF NONSENSE

'I can be quite obscure and practically marzipan.' From the macabre to the brilliantly off-beat, Mervyn Peake's nonsense verse can be enjoyed by young and old alike. This collection of writings and drawings was selected by his late widow, Maeve Gilmore, and it introduces a whole gallery of characters and creatures, such as the Dwarf of Battersea and Footfruit.

'Deserves a place among the eccentrics of the English tradition alongside Sterne, Blake, Lear, Carroll and Belloc.' – *The Times*

0 7206 1163 6   £7.95

Edith Piaf
MY LIFE

Taped shortly before her death, this is the dramatic and often tragic story of the legendary French singer Edith Piaf. She recalls her early years in the Paris underworld, her rise to international stardom, her long fight against alcohol and drugs, and her succession of stormy love affairs – and defiantly asserts the message of her most famous song, *Non, je ne regrette rien*.

0 7206 1111 3   £9.95

Marcel Proust
PLEASURES AND REGRETS

This was Proust's first published work, appearing when he was only twenty-five, and it consists of stories, sketches and thematic writings on a variety of subjects. The attitudes reflect many characteristics of the turn of the twentieth century, yet Proust illumined them with the unique shafts of observation and gift of analysis that he was later to perfect in *The Remembrance of Things Past*. This book is a period piece of intricate delights and subtle flavours that will be relished by the author's many admirers.

'This is the perfect introduction to Proust.' – *Punch*

0 7206 1110 5   £9.95

Joseph Roth
FLIGHT WITHOUT END

A young Austrian soldier returns home after the Great War. Having fought with the Red Army and worked as a Soviet official, he arrives back in bourgeois Vienna to find that it no longer has a place for him. His father has died and his fiancée, who had waited many years for his return, has married another man and left for Paris; there is nothing for an ex-soldier in Austria at the end of the Habsburg empire. He travels Europe searching in vain for a place to belong. This is the story of a young man's alienation and his search for identity and home in a world that has changed out of all recognition from the one in which he grew up.

'Almost perfect.' — *Rolling Stone*

'A very fine writer indeed.' — Angela Carter, *Guardian*

0 7206 1068 0   £9.95

THE SILENT PROPHET

This story grew out of Roth's visit to the Soviet Union in 1926, at a time when speculation was rife about the fate of Leon Trotsky. Roth referred to this book as his 'Trotsky novel', but the experiences of the book's hero, the Trotsky-like Friederich Kargan, are also recognizably those of a less well-known Jewish outsider, – Joseph Roth himself. Not strictly a historical novel nor personal analysis, *The Silent Prophet* is a beautifully descriptive journey from loneliness into an illusory worldliness back into loneliness and a haunting study of alienation.

'A novel one should not wish to be without.' – *Guardian*

'With his striking elliptical style, which can evoke despair through real wit it would be only mildly flattering to view him as a compassionate, laconic Conrad.' – *Time Out*

0 7206 1135 0   £9.95

Natsume Soseki
THE THREE-CORNERED WORLD

A key work in the Japanese transition from traditional to modern literature, this is the story of an artist who abandons city life to wander into the mountains to meditate. But when he decides to stay at a near-deserted inn he finds himself drawn to the daughter of the innkeeper. This strange and beautiful woman is rumoured to have abandoned her husband and fallen in love with a priest at a nearby temple. The artist becomes entranced by her tragic aura and he wants to paint her. Yet, troubled by a certain quality in her expression, he struggles to complete the portrait until he is finally able to penetrate the enigma of her life. Interspersed with philosophies of both East and West, Soseki's writing skilfully blends two very different cultures in this unique representation of an artist struggling with his craft and his environment.

'Natsume Soseki is generally acknowledged to have been one of the most important writers of the modern period.'
– *Times Literary Supplement*

0 7206 1156 3   £9.95

Bram Stoker
MIDNIGHT TALES

In the last decades of the nineteenth century, the Lyceum Theatre in London was the scene for brilliant gatherings hosted by the great actor Sir Henry Irving. There Irving and his guests talked of the theatre and told strange tales of far distant places. Bram Stoker was Irving's manager during these years, and such dinner-table conversations provided him with inspiration both for his immortal classic of horror fiction, *Dracula*, and for the chilling stories in this book. Opening the collection is a terrifying encounter with a werewolf, a scene from an early draft of *Dracula*. Here, too, is 'The Squaw', Stoker's most blood-curdling short story, set in a medieval torture chamber. The theatrical world features in 'Death in the Wings', a tale of brutal revenge. Also included is the dramatic finale from the 1903 novel *The Jewel of the Seven Stars*, with its raising of a mummy from the dead, which so shocked Edwardian readers that it was later expurgated. Some of the stories in this collection have not been reprinted since their original publication, and all display the fascination with the strange and the gruesome that made Bram Stoker a master of the macabre.

'A head-on collision between horror and sexuality.' – *The Times*

'Compelling . . . strictly for vampire lovers.' – *Guardian*

0 7206 1134 2   £9.95

Tarjei Vesaas
THE BIRDS

A tale of delicate beauty and deceptive simplicity by one of the greatest Scandinavian writers of the twentieth century, *The Birds* tells the story of Mattis, who is mentally retarded and lives in a small house near a lake with his sister Hege who ekes out a modest living knitting sweaters. From time to time she encourages her brother to find work to ease their financial burdens, but Mattis's attempts come to nothing. When finally he sets himself up as a ferryman, the only passenger he manages to bring across the lake is a lumberjack, Jørgen. But, when Jørgen and Hege become lovers, Mattis finds he cannot adjust to this new situation and complications abound.

'True visionary power.' – *Sunday Telegraph*

'Beautiful and subtle.' – *Scotsman*

'A masterpiece.' – *Literary Review*

'A spare, icily humane story.' – *Sunday Times*

0 7206 1143 1   £9.95

THE ICE PALACE

This is the story of two eleven-year-old girls, Unn and Siss. Unn is about to reveal a secret, one that leads to her death in the palace of ice surrounding a frozen waterfall. Siss's struggle with her fidelity to the memory of her friend, the strange, terrifyingly beautiful frozen chambers of the waterfall and Unn's fatal exploration of the ice palace are described in prose of lyrical economy that ranks among the most memorable achievements of modern literature. Tarjei Vesaas was awarded the Nordic Council Prize for this novel.

'How simple this novel is. How subtle. How strong. How unlike any other. It is unique. It is unforgettable. It is extraordinary.' – Doris Lessing, *Independent*

'It is hard to do justice to *The Ice Palace* . . . The narrative is urgent, the descriptions relentlessly beautiful, the meaning as powerful as the ice piling up on the lake. – *The Times*

0 7206 1122 9   £9.95

Noel Virtue
THE REDEMPTION OF ELSDON BIRD

Elsdon Bird is an affectionate and imaginative child raised in a family steeped in the religious intolerance of the Christian Brethren sect. When Dad gets sacked from his city workplace for proselytizing, the Birds are forced to leave Wellington and move to a small, remote town in the north. Here the family begins to disintegrate, with Elsdon becoming a whipping boy for all his family's frustrations. Driven more and more into himself, he builds a fragile internal world maintained by conversations with cows and sheep. Yet, when a sequence of disasters finally breaks up the family, the endearing Elsdon's amazing resilience and humanity see him win through in the end. Many writers have attempted to convey the terrifying world of a sensitive child in the grip of a family bent on pathological violence, but few have brought it off with such conviction.

'Little Elsdon must be the worst-treated child in literature since Smike. But Virtue never attempts to play the violin on his reader's heartstrings. Elsdon's untarnished optimism lights the bleakest landscapes and carries him to safety.' – *Independent*

'A wonderful account of childhood that touches you to the quick with its painfully funny amalgam of misery and euphoria.' – *Mail on Sunday*

0 7206 1166 0   £8.95